MANY STONES

NOVELS BY CAROLYN COMAN

MANY STONES

Carolyn Coman

FRONT STREET

Asheville, North Carolina

2000

Coman, Carolyn.
Many stones / Carolyn Coman.—1st ed.
p. cm.
Summary: After her sister Laura is murdered in
South Africa, Berry and her estranged father travel
there to participate in the dedication of a memorial
in her name.
ISBN 1-886910-55-3 (alk. paper)
[1. South Africa—Fiction. 2. Death—Fiction.
3. Family life—Fiction.] I. Title.

PZ7.C729 Man 2000
[Fic]—dc21 00-041075

For Steven Holt

"COME IN," I SAY TO JOSH AS I TURN the key in the lock and push open the front door. He is standing right behind me; I can feel his breath on my neck. *Come in*! What am I, some kind of stupid hostess? We cross the threshold and walk into the living room. What else would he do? Of course he'll come in, the way he always does when I don't have swim practice or I skip.

He drops his backpack to the floor, flops himself down on the sofa. I keep right on going, into the kitchen. "You hungry?" I call out. "Want something?"

He says no, then a second later, "Yeah, what is there?"

I bring out a bag of nugget-shaped pretzels and a can of Diet Pepsi. Josh has crossed his feet on top of a pile of my mother's books on the coffee table. I tap the end of his boot and he lifts his feet and I slide the pile out. I wipe off a waffle of dirt that has dislodged from his boot onto the books, and set them at the far side of the table.

Then I still don't sit down next to Josh. I walk into the hallway and nudge up the thermostat. I'm cold. I'm freezing. "Wanna go in my room?" I ask him.

He doesn't answer, just shrugs and gets up, grabs the Diet Pepsi, and follows me into my bedroom. I press PLAY on the CD player, start up the music Josh brought over weeks ago that I never listen to when he's not here.

Josh has stretched out on my bed and is studying the CD liner notes. I sit down next to him, but he is in the middle, so there isn't that much room. I feel a little like a nurse, or a friend visiting someone in the hospital. I watch him keep reading.

It's all I can do to sit here, because I hate this part: getting from not touching to touching. I know it's a small enough thing, something that happens in less than a second, but more and more I seem to slam up against it, no matter how much of a running start I have, how much I tell myself *Why not* or *Come on*.

Why can't he reach up to me, take my wrist, and pull me down beside him? Sometimes he does that, makes beginning a little easier. What's wrong with him? Maybe I should take his pulse: that's a way of touching.

Josh tosses the CD case back onto my bedside table. It lands at the base of my pile of stones, the pyramid of little rocks I've collected. I got the first one at the gravesite the day of Laura's funeral—a small, smooth stone that looks like it was washed up out of the ocean, not coughed up from the ground. I rubbed it with my thumb all through the service, pushed it around inside the pocket of my winter coat. That night I put it on the table next to my bed, and the night after that when I was lying on my bed in the dark I put it on my chest. It felt right, kind of like when our cat Spooky used to settle down on my stomach while I was watching TV. Since then I've picked up stones from all over. There are always stones, once you start to look.

I wish I could tell Josh. I wish I could open my mouth and talk—say how I put the stones on me, one by one, like I am the paper and they are the paperweight and they keep me from flying off, right out the window. Tell him how I *have* to do it—move them, one by one, from the nightstand onto my body, how they start out light but add up to heavy and how they keep me weighted so I know there's something *there* to be weighted.

But I'm like the stones: dumb. As in, can't speak. I turn back to Josh. He has cupped his hands under his head, his elbows are splayed out across the pillow. The look on his face registers next to nothing.

I know the look. When Josh and I were first getting together I used to ask him all the time, so hopefully, "What are you thinking?" He practically always answered, "Nothing"—and I didn't believe him, because how can you be thinking nothing and still be awake? Sometimes he would tell me about some dopey music video he'd seen, or something he and his best friend Max did when they were high together. After the first few weeks I quit asking. He was never, ever thinking about me.

All those times he said *Nothing* he was probably telling the truth. Some people probably *can* think nothing at all, and maybe they are better off. Josh thinks it's pathetic how much time I spend thinking about my screwed-up family, about families in general. Whenever I say *Happy family*, Josh says *Happy assholes*. My thoughts aren't so great or so worth having, they're mostly garbage, I know that. But I can't think nothing.

Josh raises his eyebrows, looks up at me, and grins a little. I fold myself down next to him, and he scootches over to make room, but along the way I curl up into a ball—my head against his ribs, my feet up next to his legs, breathing into my own chest.

We lie like that for a minute, me rolled up against him.

"Max and I are definitely gonna do it," he says.

His voice sounds muffled. I lift my head. "What?"

"We're definitely starting a band," Josh says.

"Oh." So that's what he is thinking about—the band, and Max. Max goes to a private boarding school in Connecticut. I've only met him once—he and Josh stopped by and Max acted like everything belonged to him, helped himself to one of my mother's beers, asked if anyone else wanted one.

"How will you practice?" I say. It's not like Max is around most of the time.

"Vacations," Josh answers, like practicing isn't really a big deal. "We'll put it together this summer."

"That's good," I say as I tuck my head down again. The news depresses me, though; I feel left behind by it.

Josh begins tapping a beat on my back, different from the beat of the music that is playing. Probably some song he and Max will do in their band. Now I know that's where Josh is—in his band, with Max, performing.

Where should *I* go? While Josh is performing? I could go to the water I'm not swimming in, the lap I'm not completing. I can *do* that, I have floating and laps deep *inside* me. I swam for seven hours at the swimathon— the First Annual Laura Morgan Memorial Swimathon. I crossed over big-time, then; I was *gone*. And I only came out because the monitors pulled me out. They said I was having trouble lifting my arms to stroke.

It's what I love, though: how swimming can take me really, really far away. Doing laps can make me forget everything—or it's not even forgetting, it's like it never was, like nothing ever was. No anything, no *me*: the details of me, my body, whatever is in my head, my name—the whole story dissolves into the water. And I love it there—*here*—under water.

Josh's tapping on my back has blended into rubbing, his whole flat palm is moving up and down my back, along my side, slowing, lighter, near my breast. My body starts to uncurl itself, stretch out. I can let this happen *and* stay under water, too.

We start slow enough, kissing, getting kind of tucked into each other. I'm so glad I'm finally going to get warm. I really like the slow part.

I love floating the most. Laura taught me when I was five, at the Belair Swim Club, where we were members for a few summers. She was wearing an orange two-piece bathing suit with iridescent fish on it and she was beautiful and perfect standing in the blue water, holding me up and promising not to let go. She taught me close to the deep end, and she took her time.

I spread out flat on my back and did everything she

told me to, puffed my stomach up to the sky, laid my head back, relaxed. "I've got you," she kept saying, and I knew she did. I could feel her fingertips under my back, guiding me through the water, and every once in a while I'd open my eyes and look at her in her orange two-piece with her beautiful perfect teeth, then close my eyes again and get that floating feeling, and it was the best feeling in the world. I still think that.

Racing doesn't mean that much to me. Other people think I care because I do so many laps. They don't know. Everyone thought I swam as long as I did at the swimathon because of Laura, my great love for her, honoring her memory. But, really, I just didn't want to come out. Once I got started, I wanted to never, ever stop. The thought of having to surface, pull my body out of the water, plant my feet on the cement, hear and see everyone around me clapping—*that's* what kept me in the water.

Josh is starting to kiss me too hard. It hurts my mouth; my lips are jammed against my teeth, our tongues act like they're furious with each other. We're already entwined, like seaweed. Seaweed in the water, in the ocean with the warm spots and the cold spots and the push of the waves.

We roll over suddenly and Josh's arm smacks the

table and the CD case falls on the floor and the pyramid collapses some, a few stones drop. It stops us momentarily: we pull apart to see what has happened, what has fallen down, and then go back to each other. I try to submerge again, into the water I am not swimming in.

But I can't—dissolve, cross over to that other place. Sometimes I get blocked, like when Dad all of a sudden shows up at swim practice. It's like he *owns* swimming now that he organized the swimathon and turned it into such a big deal. And his showing up changes everything. It totally breaks my concentration. Even when I'm under water, lapping away, I can tell that he has appeared, standing there in the humid pool air, in his business suit, for God's sake. His *business* suit. His presence pollutes the water, how the water feels to me, how I pull along inside it, the weight of my body. It adds more weight than I can carry. And then the swimming becomes nothing but effort, gets me nowhere that I care about getting to.

I press my hands against Josh's chest and push away. I tell him, "You *have* to go." Such a far cry from *Come in*! "My mom will be home soon," I say. I see that he is hurt—he startles and then runs his hand over the top of his head—but I look away. All I know is that he has to go. That suddenly, that surely. Go!

I lead him to the door. He has a rumpled, little-boy look that makes me sad. But I don't stop and I don't linger at the door. I tell him I'll see him tomorrow and I close the door behind him and I lock it. Back in my room I make the stupid, thumping music stop, then flop down onto my bed. I lift one stone off the pyramid and hold it against my chest. I won't do the whole pile; there isn't time. Mom really will be home soon. And I don't need to. I know exactly where I am: here. And I am not about to fly off. I'm here, in the house, alone. And that sound I'm hearing is the refrigerator. It's the refrigerator running.

Actually, it's the clock in the hallway, making that sound. Whatever it is, it's only a house sound, nothing to be afraid of, I'm sure I locked the door behind Josh. And Mom will be home soon.

Mom's schedule never changes. It's Dad who appears out of nowhere, unexpectedly. When he came to school to tell me about Laura, he showed up at my biology lab, and I saw him through the little rectangle of glass in the door. I knew it was him, but his face looked rearranged or something. And after I got up and went out in the hallway with him and he walked me over to underneath the stairs and started telling me—*Laura is dead, she's been killed, she was murdered*—then I couldn't look at his face at all, because it was so demolished, cracking, like his features were going to slide off onto his neck or sink inside his skull from some crushing pain that you couldn't see but was all over him. So I looked down at his feet instead, his shoes, and his pants leg, which was fluttering, shaking, like a sail or a flag in the wind.

And then, for *days* afterward, he set up camp at the house—practically moved back in with Mom and me, as if we were still the perfect family, as if he hadn't checked out years before. All of a sudden he's there in our living room, pouring drinks from a big bottle of bourbon, taking calls, making decisions, running the show the way he always does. He never stopped: making arrangements to have Laura's body flown back from South Africa, endlessly talking to reporters and embassy people because it was such a big international deal. And Mom—mute, on the couch, her hands folded.

The phone rang constantly, and each time my father *dove* to answer it. He lunged for it, shot his big body off the couch to get it, jolted away from conversations, drink in hand, to take the calls. As if they could make a difference, change something.

After the funeral and the reception, Mom got up off the sofa and told Dad that it was over. She put her hand on his arm when she said it, and then he left again. Dead is dead, that's when I started to know.

But even after that, I had to keep reminding myself that dead is forever—she's still dead, she's dead again, she's always dead, she's dead from now on—until I finally got it. I don't know if Dad gets it yet or not. He's still busy doing stuff: setting up the swimathon, arranging for this memorial to Laura over in South Africa.

I never believed for one second that all the laps in the world could change anything. And I don't buy that Laura is somewhere watching, approving, feeling not forgotten because her old high school swim team lapped their hearts out for her. I don't know what happens to you after you die, but it doesn't make sense to me that you see or feel or know things the same way you do when you are alive. Maybe you don't see or know or experience anything in any way at all, but I doubt you care a whole lot about high school swimathons. I hope death isn't that lame, as lame as all the rest of us who are left behind.

I hear Mom's car in the driveway. A snippet of *All Things Considered* flies out into the air before the car turns off. Even though I can't see her, I see her: reaching into the back seat and lifting out the bag of books she always lugs around, coming up the walk. My mother teaches kids who think they can't learn to read to read.

I only have a second to decide whether to spring up and greet her or lie here and wait for her to find me. I jump up and get to the front door as she is pushing it open.

"Hi, Berry," she calls out before she sees me, and then, when she does, "Oh. Hi, darling."

"Hi, Mom." She looks tired, what we call *all read out.*

"How are you?" she says to me. She is hanging up her coat and storing her bag of books in the hall closet. She turns her attention to my face and reads *me*, takes me in. I don't know what or how much shows. "Are you all right?" she says.

I nod. She strokes the side of my face, my cheek. I feel bad about Josh coming over after school. Not because she doesn't know, or because we fool around. There's just something sad about it. She'd hate me adding more sadness.

"So what shall we do about dinner?" she says, and we both go into the kitchen. I pull out a stool from under the counter, and she opens the refrigerator and peers in, starts moving stuff around to see what's there. She pulls out some containers and stacks them by the sink. We'll have leftovers and they'll be fine, or if I want to make myself macaroni and cheese or plain noodles, she'll let me. Even cold cereal is OK. We never argue about food anymore. I can't believe we ever did.

"How's Leroy?" I ask her. Her back is to me, she's still bent over, and I see again how different our bodies are: hers short and squat and me such a string bean. Leroy is this boy she's been tutoring who I met last week.

Josh was supposed to come home with me that day, but then he couldn't, and when I got to the house I couldn't make myself go inside alone. I actually stood on the doorstep with the key in my hand and looked at the door and couldn't do it—let myself in and be home alone.

So I went over to Mom's school instead. I used to go there every day after Mom and I first moved to Rockville, after the divorce. She made me. She said I was too young to be home alone after school. Now I am not too young and now is when I cannot do it. Isn't it ironic? Back then she had a little room set up for me— a closet, really—where I could do my homework and be out of the way while she did her tutoring.

When I showed up last week she was scared, at first. "Is everything all right?" she blurted out. It's what she— and Dad, now, too—says whenever the slightest thing is different. But as soon as I told her that I just felt like coming over, the way I used to, then she was really pleased.

"Well, I'm *so* glad," she said, and I felt like I'd made her happy by accident, because I'd been scared to be home alone. "Now you can meet Leroy, and Leroy can meet you. Leroy, this is my daughter, Berry. Berry is my daughter who loves to read comic books."

Leroy, a deep-brown boy with big circle eyes, looked at me, shy, for an instant.

"Berry, this is Leroy. The Leroy I've told you about. My shining student. A star." I could see Leroy smile, though he didn't raise his face again. "And we've found important information about Leroy's name in this book we've been reading together." She tapped the book that lay open between the two of them. "What Leroy's name *means*," she said.

My mother loves her work. It's almost like she climbs inside it to sit beside some kid who she *knows* is going to read. I've heard her so many times, moving sounds and letters and words off the pages of the books she totes around, into kids' heads, kid after kid after kid. She has done this for years and years. *Sound it out, take a guess, good!*

I hoped Leroy would take his cue, that my mother wouldn't have to prod him into telling me. He looked up and cocked his head. "The king," he said, nodding a little. "Leroy means the king."

. . .

"Leroy is magnificent," my mother says, turning to me, Tupperware in hand. "He is so pleased with himself he is bursting." Leroy, who, in the first week my mother worked with him, was so frustrated about not reading that he bit her.

"So," she says to me, "beef stroganoff, green beans, leftover Chinese."

I choose Chinese. I'm glad she's home. Things are what they are when she's around. It's not like Laura didn't die and we're pretending. It's like: Laura died and we have what we have and here we are. Leftovers, Leroy, Josh gone until tomorrow.

We make dinner and check the TV to see if anything good is on.

She asks me, in passing, how swimming was.

"OK," I say. Then, "Actually I skipped today." I can't not tell her too many things. I know that to be with her and have it feel all right, have it be some kind of *relief,* I have to keep things pretty up to date.

"Why?" she asks.

"I didn't ... couldn't. Get there," I finish.

She looks at me for a moment. I know it's not the swimming she cares about.

"Do you want to stay on the team?" she asks after a while, a real question.

I shrug. "I don't know," I say.

My mother nods and doesn't say anything else, doesn't ask me to know more than I do.

She turns on a PBS special about breakthroughs in pharmaceutical treatment of the mentally ill. I only watch a little, and then I tell her I'll be in my room.

My father calls as I'm drifting off. He wants to wish me luck at the swim meet tomorrow, to let me know he will be there. He has rearranged his schedule so that he can be there. It's so weird, all his sudden attention to me and my swimming. None of it feels like it has anything to do with me, really. It's more like I am Dad's new hobby or cause.

"Oh," I say. "OK." Not the most gracious response, but the best I can do. What I really want to do is go to sleep.

"I have high hopes," he tells me. I bet he does. He's always had them. He had them big-time for Laura. If he's transferring them to me he'll be sorry. I'm not Laura, in case he hasn't noticed. And I don't share them, his high hopes. It's all I can do, really, the only power I have, *not* to share them, not to feed his dream of how things are when I know they aren't. "You get your sleep now," he says.

Even telling me to sleep well sounds like he is giving me an order.

I get a late start in the race. I'm off, but I was off before we left the locker room, before I ever changed into my suit. It's like I'm a beat behind myself and there's no way to catch up. Even my thoughts are slow and heavy. Even that I'm aware of *thinking* them is off! I should be slicing, cutting, sharking through the water. Things should be fast instead of slow, and they're not. I should not be watching myself from behind, but I am. And it comes to me, slowly, clearly, from behind, that I am out of this race. Oh, I really am.

I keep swimming, but now that I *know*, there's no *not* knowing. I am swimming a race that has nothing to do with me. My pace slows. The lap I'm swimming becomes simply a lap, all on its own, one of a thousand, one that has nothing to do with anyone else—only me and the water.

I make it to the wall, flip under, and kick off, but all in slower motion than anything that's going on around me. Gliding up through the water, my body turns. And by the time I surface I am on my back. Floating. The triangular metal rafters of the ceiling are above me, and the lights. The noise of everything is still half under water. I spread out my arms. I arch my back, my stomach rises up as if there's an invisible string pulling it to the sky. And now I close my eyes. For the remaining seconds I have, before the race is really over and I have to come out, again, to anything that's left, I float. Perfectly, until I can almost feel the tips of Laura's fingers on my back. *I've got you, relax, I've got you.*

My father is waiting outside the locker room. He has to know, right away, if I'm all right, what happened, am I sick.

Yes, nothing, no.

"It wasn't my race," is what I tell him, all I know.

He insists on giving me a ride home, even though there is a late bus I can take. I have told the coach I am quitting the team, but my father doesn't know that yet. He still thinks there is hope.

We walk out to the parking lot and climb into his cushy baby-blue Saab. He is a big man; he rocks the car as he positions himself behind the wheel. He is readying himself to convince me that I want to do what he wants me to do—compete. It's his job, getting people to see things his way: Dad is a lobbyist. It makes me sick how he thinks Laura was so much like him, that she followed in his footsteps because she chose international studies and human rights to work in. As if they did the same thing. Dad's all business.

I open the window a crack. I lean over and turn on the radio and find the station that Josh listens to, and a second later Dad lowers the volume and starts in. He talks about keeping up with my racing because it is all I have. Not those words exactly, but I know that's what he means. "And if you *do* give up swimming," he says, "what will you replace it with?"

"What?"

"Where will you direct your time and energy?" he asks. "Have you thought about that?"

What energy? I wonder. "Not really," I say.

"You might want to," he says, hopeful now that I am with him, on board for whatever it is he is telling me. "You don't want to—can't really afford to—let go of too many things."

I don't say *Why not.*

"It's important to hold on to things and follow through, not let them slide one by one."

"Oh," I say. The sliding. That. My grades, my attitude, my appearance. Dad hates what is left of my hair. "You mean the hollow shell of my life without swimming?"

Dad takes his eyes off the road and looks at me. His face changes, his mouth sets. He sees that I am not on board after all.

He is quiet for a while. What, I wonder, does he think swimming *is* in my life, exactly? The chance to win, I suppose. So? Anything'll give you that. And who *cares* if you win? Or lose?

"I don't find your attitude particularly helpful," he finally says.

Right, Dad. "I quit the team," I tell him.

When we get home I pull back the door handle before he comes to a complete stop. "Thanks," I say, ready to hop out, but he turns off the car and comes up to the house with me. I wish he wouldn't; he so doesn't belong here, where Mom and I live.

Mom is sitting at the kitchen table paying bills when we walk in. "Judith," my father says, grim, as if he is announcing her name for the record.

She keeps her eyes on me. "Are you all right?" she asks, and when I tell her I am, just tired, she lets it drop. Mom doesn't beat things to death. She doesn't ask about the race and how it went. I guess I don't have *winner* written all over me.

I go into my room, lie on my bed and cross my legs

at the ankles, look up at my ceiling. I can hear my mother and father talking in that weird, I-don't-know-you voice they have for each other. Dad is breaking the bad news, I know, telling what I did and outlining suggestions for how to handle the situation.

Their voices get quieter and more serious than ever. I reach over and take the top stone off the pile on my bedside table, place it on my chest. My parents go back and forth with each other, and I transfer the pile of stones, one by one.

They talk an awfully long time, for them. They usually keep it short and to the point, what weekends I'll be with whom, now that Dad has moved back to Washington. Mostly they do it by phone. Tonight they're going on and on: I have the entire pile of stones transferred and resting on my chest, heavy as a fat, sleeping cat.

I actually can't believe Mom is buying into the great tragedy of me quitting the swim team. She doesn't care about sports. She has told me a bunch of times that she had enough of high school and college sports (meaning my father's) to last her a lifetime.

Now I wish I had told her the news myself, instead of letting Dad. I gave away my chance to go first. Or my father took it by following me into the house. Whatever I say now will be polluted by his version. Like that game where something gets whispered around a whole circle, and the last person to hear it says it out loud and it's completely different—completely wrong—from how it started out.

So what *is* my version? I floated because I am done with swimming and the race was already over. I don't care about it anymore and my body knows it. I floated because I had to.

Of course my timing could have been better. I could have floated at practice instead of a meet. Or done it without my father watching in the stands, away from his important meetings rearranged for my sake. My timing was totally off, I guess. And timing is everything, right? It can make all the difference in the world: where you are any given second of the day, instead of being someplace else. You hear those stories of people who miss their plane and then that plane crashes, and if they hadn't been stuck in traffic they would have died, too. Or people who are visiting a place for the first and only time, and it gets blown up, some bomb. Timing. If one little thing had been different, one minor change in the schedule, Laura probably wouldn't be dead. Wrong time, wrong place—a lot of people said that afterward, when Laura was already dead forever, murdered, and there was no chance of making any of those tiny adjustments that might have made all the difference.

Finally I hear my father leave. I feel the full weight of the pile of stones on my chest, rising and lowering minutely with my breath. They don't make breathing easier, but they are comforting all the same.

I want to get up and go out and talk to Mom, but I can't.

Not too much later, she comes to me, knocks on my door. I roll over and the stones all slide off me into a heap by my side. "Come in."

"Hungry?" she asks me, standing in the doorway, looking at me.

I tell her I'll get a bowl of cereal in a few minutes. I wait for her to ask me what happened.

And wait. Mom has all this patience, it's from teaching reading. Or maybe she teaches reading because she had patience to begin with.

I finally give in. "Dad told you what happened?"

"Mmm," she says. "He did. And you've decided to leave the team."

Leave now *there's* a nicer word than quit. Unlike deceased, or passed away, which people use instead of dead, but isn't any better at all. "Yeah," I say.

"Yes," she says. "He told me."

And? So? "What," I say. I feel ridiculous, like I am forcing her to examine me.

"Well, darling," she says, "I assume you've thought this through. Are you not sure?"

"No," I say. "I'm definitely done."

"Well, it's *your* decision," she says. And then, "The floating, though. An interesting exit." We both chuckle; I am not exactly sure why. And even though she is smiling, she looks sad to me. I don't know how I look. She doesn't say anything else and clearly isn't going to.

"So what were you and Dad talking about for so long?" I ask.

She gets very still. "I got a fax from Laura's school in Cape Town this afternoon," she says. The school where Laura was volunteering when she got killed. "The memorial is done, and they have set the date for the ceremony."

It's odd, lying here and having her tell me this. I'm listening, but all I'm waiting for is where it's going.

"Next month, at the school. And Daddy is definitely planning to attend."

It always sounds weird to me, her saying *Daddy*.

I am watching her, waiting.

"He wants you to go, too, darling. He thinks it would be a good idea for you to go with him."

Bingo—so that's what this conversation is really about.

"Why didn't he ask *me*?" I say. "Why is he telling *you*?"

"It came to him, Berry, when we were talking. Of course he'll ask you. I'm telling you because you asked what we were talking about."

Her answer isn't good enough. I feel exploded inside.

"Berry," my mother says, "he's concerned about what your response will be. He doesn't feel that you give him many ways in."

"And so, what? He invites me through you and that's supposed to smooth things over?"

"He's *trying*, Berry. Trying is what people often do prior to getting it right."

This must be something Mom says to her kids when she is teaching them to read. Or something she says to herself so she can stand to keep going over the same stuff again and again.

I can't believe she's on his side. "So how does this work?" I ask her. "Do I tell you what I think and you tell him? What will happen if you're not around to relay the messages back and forth?"

She smiles. "You'll manage quite nicely without me, I'm sure."

I'm not sure. About anything. Unlike my father, who

is sure about almost everything, positive that whatever he does or pays attention to is worth it.

"I think it's a good idea, Berry," my mother says.

I can tell that she means it. I feel a little scared. "If you think it's such a good idea, then why don't you come too?"

As soon as I've said it, I'm sorry. I know she can't. Would never.

She says, "I can't leave my kids." And it's true enough, but not the reason. The real reason is that when Laura died my mother lost a ring out of herself, a ring like a tree has—something that ran all the way around her and touched every other part. She operates on less, now, because there is less in her. She does what's in front of her—me, and her kids who are learning to read—but not what's behind or around her, not memorial statues or swimathons. South Africa is way too *far* for her to go.

Not to mention that she and Dad are divorced, and strangers.

"I was *kidding*, Mom," I tell her. "I'm not really suggesting a family reunion in South Africa."

She has this slightly dazed look, like she was momentarily caught.

I know she could never go. I just don't know about me.

". . ."

"Let's talk about our trip to South Africa," Dad says, when he finally gets around to bringing it up. We are having lunch at a restaurant in Dupont Circle. It's my weekend with him. "How you want to work it," he says. I guess that's the question part—how I want to work it—not whether or not I'll be going.

He tells me the dates and places we'll be visiting. He says something about a national park and wild animals. He tells me we'll meet Father Alan, the man Laura worked most closely with at the school. He tells me that he'd like me to present the check with all the money we raised from the swimathon. I'm wondering what could possibly be left to decide.

"What about school," I say halfheartedly. "Won't I miss a lot?"

"Four days," he says, ready with an answer. The trip, it turns out, dovetails nicely with my February break.

"Oh," I answer. "So what else is there? To work out?"

"Well, these are only suggestions I have," he says. He is nervous—suddenly I see that, and it surprises me because why should he be? He is so in charge of everything. "I want to make sure this works for you, too," he says. "What do *you* want?"

Dad is big on wanting, mostly his own. It's always easy to tell what he wants to be doing and who he wants to be doing it with: just look at what he's doing and who he's doing it with. Most of the time I was growing up it was obvious he wanted to be with Laura. She was always getting awards or in a play or on a team he could brag about. And by the time she was in high school, they could talk about stuff he was interested in, they'd have these long discussions about politics and world affairs. I was still a kid. I wanted to play.

But he did buy me the bike of my dreams when I was six years old—a bright pink bicycle with striped plastic strips flying off the grips of the handlebars. My family called the color peptoabismal. And the guy at the store pointed out that even with the seat raised, it wasn't going to last me for long. What Dad kept telling me, though, was, "Get the one you want."

He is looking at me now like he's waiting for an answer, but I forgot the question.

OUR FIRST IN-FLIGHT MOVIE will be *Six Days, Seven Nights,* which I have already seen. The attendant comes down the aisle handing out headphones and my father asks for another glass of red wine instead. He has a pile of business papers on his little tray table. She smiles at him and says of course. I take the headphones and put them on right away. So far there is only Celine Dion, wailing away on the pop channel, but then Harrison Ford and Anne Heche come on, pretending to hate each other when they are obviously head over heels in love.

Dad says something to me and I pretend I can't hear him. He taps me on the arm to get my attention. I pull back one ear of my headphones.

"Did you read about the controversy around this movie?" he asks me. Harrison Ford and Anne Heche are on top of a cliff, about to hit each other or kiss or both. "She's a lesbian," he says, not taking his eyes off the screen for a second.

I look at my father—*She's a lesbian*—and any thought, any stupid hope I had that this trip might actually work out for us, vanishes, right out the window, poof. I drop the earphone like a plug down over my ear. "So *what*?" I say and push back in my seat. I wonder if he says stuff like that in meetings, to the people he works with, do they talk like that too? He continues to watch the screen, papers sprawled across his tray table, no headphones, for as long as she's standing there wearing practically nothing.

There's no movie during dinner, so I have to unplug. I check the in-flight magazine and see that movie #2 is *Titanic*. Before I stop myself I point it out to my father, and we both laugh.

"Questionable programming for a transatlantic flight," he says, and all of a sudden I'm sorry I gave him an in. I don't ask if he remembers that song I learned in first grade, and loved so much, about the *Titanic: Husbands and wives, little children lost their lives ... it was sad, so sad, it was sad, sad, sad.* It was such a chirpy little tune! I used to lie in bed and really belt it out to Laura, and she always laughed and sometimes sang along with me. She was the one who told me that it was a pretty twisted little ditty.

The flight attendants pass out steaming washcloths with tongs so we can wipe our hands and faces. The cloths are burning hot at first but almost instantly turn clammy. Over dinner Dad starts telling me about the work he'll be doing in Johannesburg. I wipe the cherries in slime off my cheesecake and barely listen. But when he says that "the blacks are in a very tough negotiating position," I correct him. "African-Americans," I say. I can't believe he still says *blacks*.

He stops for a second, fork halfway up to his mouth. "Not in South Africa," he says. "Blacks in South Africa—as they are called, and call themselves—aren't at all American."

"Oh, yeah," I say, and my face starts to pulse. I hate it when I say something stupid around him. Now we're even: his Anne Heche comment, me being wrong about blacks.

When it actually comes time for the next movie I don't know about watching all those frozen dead people floating in the ocean again, fond as I am of floating.

Besides, I hate how much people cry at *Titanic*. I would never cry at that movie. Even the thought of crying over it makes me mad. People cried forever when Laura died. I decide to sleep instead of watching the movie; I stuff pillows next to the window and lean against them.

When I wake up there is nothing on the screen and the cabin is all dark except for a few overhead reading lamps and the runway of lights along the base of the seats. My body is stiff from having slept crooked and my teeth feel a little furry. I shrink past my sleeping father and head for the bathroom.

On my way back to my seat I look at our projected route on the movie screen. The plane is a green dot that is moving forward even as I watch it, making an arc toward Cape Verde, our only stop—to refuel—before Johannesburg. Mom is back home where she belongs and I am going farther away every minute. It makes me feel a little sick.

Dad wakes up as I try to slide past him. "You OK?" he blurts out first thing, before he's completely awake, and it makes me mad.

"Yes, I'm all right," I say to him. My words come out in slices. "I just went to the bathroom."

He doesn't say anything else, and I know I snapped at him, but I couldn't help it. I hate that scared look of his.

"Not too much longer now," he says to me, leaning

in, and his old face is back—set, in charge. I can't stand that look, either.

When we step off the plane in Cape Verde, the air is not hot, not cold, not refreshing, hardly air at all. Like it's not even a real place. It feels so weird to be up in the middle of the night and not with one of my friends or at a party or in my own room, and here I am on some runway, on some island, walking toward some terminal building in the dark. All of a sudden it hits me: Where *am* I? What am I *doing*? All these people are filing out of the plane around us and I sneak looks at them and they all seem completely blank. I wonder how they can stand to be here, why none of them are crying. And then I *make* myself think about the *Titanic* so *I* don't cry.

A driver from the hotel where we'll be staying for the first few days meets us at the airport when we get to Johannesburg. He's thin, beautiful, black, looks about my age. He is standing in his uniform, holding up a cardboard sign with our name on it: Morgan. He is wearing a royal blue cap with a strap underneath that reminds me of Curious George.

As soon as we get into the van, Dad starts interviewing him. I know he is asking the questions partly for my benefit, so that I can make the most of this trip, learn all about the population of Soweto, or politics, or what the driver thinks of Nelson Mandela. My father asks how long he has worked at the hotel.

"At Hedgecliff, sir, I have worked three months."

"How's it going for you? Do you like it?"

I can tell our driver hates it. Like he probably hates that stupid cap he has to wear. But it's his job. He answers all my father's questions but never says more than he has to.

"Do you live in Johannesburg?"

My father will go on like this forever.

I push against the corner of the back seat where the driver can't see me in the rear-view mirror but where I can see the curl of his eyelashes against his eyelids and, when he adjusts the mirror, his pink palms. His face, which is perfect, shows nothing.

I wonder what it would be like to kiss a black man. And if it's OK to wonder that, or if it's racist. Or sexist. I wonder if he would ever wonder that about me. Or if he only hates us.

"And where did you go to school?" my father asks.

. . .

Finally we pull up a long, winding driveway to an en-closed village of chalets and lodges and kidney-shaped swimming pools. The grass is so green it looks fake; we could be at Disney World.

In the main lobby, the jittery white man who seems to be in charge comes out from behind the desk to tell us what a great pleasure it is to welcome us to Hedge-cliff. He squeezes out the word so that it comes out as *plee-zure*. He is so anxious to please that he is practi-cally vibrating, standing in front of us, between two zebra-striped ottomans. "Please follow me," he says. "Right this way." He treats us like we're some kind of different species who must never be troubled or made to wait or inconvenienced in any way. I can feel my father loving it, all the attention.

We have a suite, Dad and I—two bedrooms and a lit-tle sitting room in the middle, loaded with plump chairs and couches. At the bathroom door Peter, our eager guide, pauses to point out the telephones—two of them—and the switch on the wall that controls the heated towel rack. The end of the toilet paper roll is folded in a perfectly formed V.

Suddenly Peter's face pinches up. He leans in and flips on the switch. "This *should* have been turned on prior to your arrival," he says, clearly perturbed. I don't know what he's talking about, but then he says, "It will take a few minutes before your towels are properly warmed. I *do* apologize." My father raises his hand and gives his head a little shake: no problem.

I watch Peter and my father make nice about the stupid heated towel rack not having been turned on. They could be doing a Monty Python skit, especially with Peter's snippy little accent. But no one is laughing. "Gee, I don't know, Dad," I say—it slips out of me—"I wanted to take a shower *right away.*"

My father gives me a look, a *Don't start, Berry* look. "You'll live," he says dryly. Peter quivers more than ever. He is caught between my father and me momentarily, but then he goes with Dad, of course—the man, the adult, the one who's paying—and the tour of our suite continues. Peter is showing us the TV console that rises up out of the floor of our living room. Laura would have hated this place. She would *never* have stayed here.

"So, how are you doing?" my father asks me as soon as he has ordered his scotch and soda. We have come to the plumped-up lounge for a bite to eat. Our arrival has set off a little commotion of serving: waiters draping the table in front of us with a starched white cloth and laying out silverware and glasses. Dad's question is full of hope, as if twenty-four hours in his company might already have begun to do the trick in turning me around.

"The same," I tell him, level as the floor. "I'm the same."

He considers my response, weighs whether to pursue or retreat. Every conversation is a skirmish.

I want to disappear into our overstuffed chairs. I wish I could signal to the black men who are doing all the serving that I don't really belong here, I just got brought along.

"The same as what?" he asks politely, and then takes a sip of his scotch.

"The same as always," I say. It really is funny how he thinks Laura was like him. I'm the one who's like him. Or can be. I can be hard the way he is. And cold. What my mother calls a stinker, or a dirty bird. I can give back what I get: very little.

He shrugs, turns the corners of his mouth down a bit. "I'd say there have been a *few* changes over the years," he says.

I don't want to talk anymore. "I guess," I say, and hope that that will hold him and our food will come soon.

It doesn't. "Laura's death certainly changed many things for all of us," he says.

The tablecloth is bright white linen, not a wrinkle in

it. My knife and fork and spoon lie polished on top of it—bright, distorting little mirrors. Laura dying, getting killed, having her head smashed open with a rock changed many things. I put my hand over the heavy knife and slide it back and forth across the tablecloth. I see Mom sliding down the kitchen wall with the phone still in her hand, crying as she tries to tell my aunt. Laura's death was a definite change for all of us.

"And I know it's been awfully hard for you, this last year and a half without her."

"Dad," I break in, "can we not talk about this right now? We just got here and I'm really tired and all I want to do is have dinner and go to bed."

"Of course," he says, and I see that I've hurt him and also that he's a little mad, and I want to pick up my glass of ice water and throw it in his face, to erase what I see.

When I finally do go to bed I can't sleep, and in the morning I'm wrecked. Dad says he didn't sleep either, but he is showered and shaved and straightening his tie in the sitting room mirror, ready to go off to his scheduled business meeting. He explains to me again that it's not safe for me to go anywhere outside the hotel grounds on my own. Crime is out of control here, especially in Johannesburg. I know that the country where my sister got killed is dangerous. He says I can swim, or read, or sleep. He tells me to sign for anything I need, and for a second I don't know what he's talking about. Sign for what I need: I picture one of those signers for the deaf, making fast hand movements. "The room number," he says, eyebrows up, nodding slowly at me, and when I finally get what he means I laugh at how I'd misunderstood. I see him stiffen. He hates it when I laugh and he doesn't know why, probably thinks I'm laughing at him.

"I'll see you later, then," he tells me as he walks out the door.

As soon as the door clicks shut behind him, I'm sorry that he's gone because I am alone. But what am I going to do, throw open the door and run after him? Call out *I'm sorry*? For what? I run my fingers through my short head of hair and squeeze until my scalp hurts. I swear out loud, tromp back to the bedroom.

I crawl into bed and pull the covers over my head and make a dark, stuffy cocoon that I warm with my own breath. I sleep like that until there is a knock on the door—housekeeping—to see if I want the room made up.

I get dressed and go walking around the hotel property. Vans roam the road, looking to see if anybody wants to go anywhere. I wave them on, since I'm only out for a walk, but I check to see if it might be our beautiful driver from yesterday. Would I take a ride from him? I'd have to say where I wanted to go and what I wanted to do, and I don't know that.

I end up by the thumb-shaped pool nearest to our building, perfect for dipping. It's strange to sit beside the water and not be in it. There's no way, from the outside, to understand what it's like to be submerged, how totally sealed it is once you're under. From here it's all that cool Edward Hopper blue, like eye hypnosis. And inside, it's everything, all there is.

But I don't want to get in, not here. There's not enough room to really swim, barely enough to float. I know it's heated to avoid a single goose bump. But sitting beside the pool is weird, too, like I'm pretending to have a different life from the one I have. All I am really doing is waiting for Dad to get back, which I hate.

When Mom and he split up—I was twelve, Laura was already away at college—I waited a year for him to come back. Mom told me he was not going to, but Dad never said anything at all, which I took to mean that he might. Even after he moved to California I kept waiting. About six months after he moved he came back to Washington on business and said he had something important to tell me. He took me out to a fancy restaurant. Over salad he said, "I know that you and your mother have probably already talked about this, but we have decided to call it quits." Over dessert he told me about Martina, the woman he was living with in San Francisco.

Dad is in high business mode when he gets back. I can tell because he registers my presence with a little jolt of surprise, as if he'd forgotten that he brought me with him, that we're here together for our big, important father-daughter trip. He's still in whatever meeting he just got out of.

He does his best, though. "Well, how did *your* day go?" he asks. I think we sound like a sit-com. *Oh, fine, dear. I sat by the pool. But the kids were naughty and I want you to spank them all very, very hard.*

I say my day went fine and he starts to tell me all about the meeting and the economic strategy and what this newly formed group is up against. He invites me to go with him to the lounge so he can get a drink, and though I have been waiting all day for him to get back, waiting and waiting and waiting, when he asks me to join him, *no* hops out of my mouth fast as a cricket.

"Oh, come on," he says, giving me the chance to change my mind. I flick it back at him.

"I already ate."

He shrugs. "Well, then," he says, "I'll be back in a while." Maybe he feels guilty, leaving me again right away, because as he's going out the door he tells me that if I feel like calling home I should go ahead.

It takes me a while to figure out how the phone works and get the right country code, but I do, and then I dial Josh's number. He answers on the first ring, and I'm not ready, can't quite take it in—that I could so quickly be in touch with someone so far away. "Josh?" I say. "Josh? It's Berry."

There is a pause—all the thousands of miles between us, or his surprise, or how stoned he probably is—and then he says, "Berry! Berry good! Berryberryberry."

He's stoned. Even from so far away I can tell. "How are you?" I ask. *How are you.* Things are already stupid.

He tells me all about the concert he and James went to, how great it was, and the new CD he got, can I hear it, and I can see him lying on his bed in his room, holding the phone out to the air and letting the music pound through the wires—some guy, screaming—to where I am lying on this enormous hotel bed. And all of a sudden the disappearing feeling comes over me, like the particles of me are starting to evaporate one by one. The guy on the CD goes on and on, yelling words

I can't understand. Finally Josh comes back on the line. "Like it?" he says.

"Mmm," I say, hear myself say. "I'm in Africa, Josh," I blurt out, to try and make something clear.

"I *know*," he says. "Lions and tigers and bears, lions and tigers and bears."

"Right," I say. "I have to go," I tell him. "I was just checkin' in."

"Great," he says, "good. Hey, when you comin' back?"

I told him so many times. I tell him again.

The night of some concert, it turns out. "Too bad," he says. I'll miss it.

My father returns after about an hour. I haven't moved off the bed. "Call home?" he asks.

"Yeah," I tell him. "I called Josh."

"Josh?" I can hear how wrong wrong wrong my answer is. Dad has met Josh twice and obviously thinks he is a loser.

"Yeah," I say. "Josh."

He comes to stand in the doorway of my room. He is such a big man. His shoes are very soft leather. "You called Josh?" he repeats.

I wonder how many times we can go back and forth saying Josh's name, which one of us will give up first. I do. "Yes," I say. But then I change my mind and add, "Josh."

He purses his lips and considers what he is going to say next. "Berry, when I suggested calling home, it wasn't Josh I had in mind."

I don't miss a beat. "Well then, when *you* call home, don't call Josh." Being with my father is making me faster, honing my edge.

"You're awfully comfortable taking advantage of the luxuries you have such disdain for," he says.

"Dad, you *told* me I could call home." My voice is loud. Now I sound like a baby. I get a good line in sometimes, but I never stay level with him.

"*Home*, Berry. Your *mother*. I thought she might appreciate knowing how you were doing, hearing from you."

I know that. I knew that. I knew he meant I should call Mom. "Well, you didn't *say* Mom, you said *home*. There are a lot of people back home. I didn't know I had to call the one you were thinking of."

What I say, even though I don't believe it, seems to make some sort of impression on him, and he backs off a little, sighs.

I sit up on the bed and look down at the carpet, bounce my feet. I couldn't call Mom. I couldn't stand to hear her voice so far away. Maybe later in the trip, but not from this place, after a day outside the water, waiting for Dad to come back, inching toward Laura once and for all and forever. Mom's voice would kill me. *Darling. Oh, Berry. Tell me, how is it?* It had to be Josh. I can count on Josh, really count on him, for so little.

My father tells me that he has scheduled a tour of Soweto. Peter, at the front desk, has taken care of all the arrangements.

"Are you kidding?" I say. "A tour?" Like driving around Washington, D.C., to look at poor people and slummy buildings? I think maybe he is having another *She's a lesbian* moment. Or maybe I have it wrong. I can't remember what Laura said about Soweto. Those weren't the parts of her letters that mattered to me. "Isn't Soweto the really poor place?" I check.

He looks at me a moment before answering, to make sure that I am serious about not knowing. "Where the struggle against apartheid was born?" he says, so sure he can jog my social-studies memory. "The riots in '76? When the schoolchildren were shot? Home of Desmond Tutu? Winnie Mandela?"

I keep looking at him, don't even blink, so close to saying that it's hard to believe I am Laura's sister, isn't it?

"And no," he says, "I am not kidding about the tour." He is loosening his necktie and unbuttoning the top button of his shirt.

"Fine," I say, and go into my bedroom and close the door.

I kneel down and reach for my shoes under the bed and remember the first Christmas Laura came home from college after Mom and Dad had split up. Dad and I picked Laura up at the airport, and then Dad took us out to dinner at the Press Club in Washington, his favorite place. I was so sad when Laura automatically climbed in the front next to him and they right away got into some big discussion about whether Americans should invest in South African companies. I watched the back of Laura's head—she'd gotten her hair cut, and her neck looked so different to me—and her profile when she turned to him: "Dad, it's morally *indefensible*."

I could feel how much Dad *loved* discussing politics with Laura, even though they were arguing. And it was so clear to me that Laura had gone over and been welcomed into territory I didn't know anything about. I felt a thousand miles down the road from where she and Dad were, up front, with the steering wheel and all the lights and controls on the panel of the dashboard.

That night Laura sat with me in back on the way home, French-braided my hair, asked me about my friends at school. Dad referred to himself as James, the chauffeur, but I knew there was no catching up.

And I know there's no not going to Soweto. I lace up my boots and check myself in the mirror, but I'm not sure what to wear for our tour of the ghetto.

"All set?" Dad asks when I emerge. He is ready to start over with me, from scratch.

I have never been surrounded by so many black people in my life—*all* black people, because not one white person lives in Soweto. Mr. Joseph Otambo, a big black man in a brightly patterned shirt, is driving us around the neighborhoods of Soweto in his mini-van. He tells us that in the huge hospital to our right, one out of three babies born has AIDS. In a neighborhood of bigger, nicer homes, he pulls over and points up to a house. "This is the home of Desmond Tutu, winner of the Nobel Peace Prize." A little while later he shows us the home where Nelson Mandela once lived. "Also a Nobel Peace Prize winner." Mr. Otambo turns and looks at my father and me and holds up two fingers in a V. "The only neighborhood in the world with two winners!" And then he gives a good laugh.

I have stopped feeling so embarrassed about being here and doing what we are doing, because Mr. Otambo sure doesn't seem to be. He points out places and tells us things, laughs a lot. I keep having this weird feeling that he is speaking another language but that I am un-derstanding it because he keeps it really simple, just says what things are.

We drive by a small school and he tells us, "This is where the schoolchildren were shot during the uprising in 1976."

At the first squatter village we come to—acres of tents and shacks pieced together with cardboard and tin and scrap planks of wood—he points to a tilting out-house in the middle of a bunch of shacks and says, "This is a toilet the people who live here use."

I sit still in the van and look at what he has stopped to show us: a decrepit outhouse, sad and exposed. It re-minds me of the latrine we had at summer camp, ex-cept the one at camp was a whole lot better. At least it was set in the woods, not in the middle of a city street, at least there was some privacy. But it was still the thing I hated the most about camp, other than being home-sick. The stink of it, and the sounds of using it, how there was no getting away from them.

"Now you can see the inside of the toilet," he says, at another narrow, broken outhouse whose door is missing. "There are not enough for all the people who live here."

Mr. Otambo invites us to go inside one of the shacks. It is part of the tour. He tells us it's all right with the woman who lives there, that people in the village want visitors to see with their own eyes what it is like for some of the people who live here in Soweto.

I don't know if it shows that I'm scared. My father leads the way out of the van, and we enter the shack closest to the road. There is a woman sitting on a cot inside. She says her name is Mary and we all shake hands and then we are silent inside the dark tent. There is a picture from a magazine taped up on the wall, but the wall is a piece of cardboard. A towel stretches across a rope to divide the space into rooms, but the whole place is no bigger than a closet to start with, no bigger than the playhouse Laura and I had behind our home in Kensington, a log cabin made little-kid size. Mary, answering my father's question, tells us she has six children.

Six kids, *six*. In this place where I am standing, crowded together with just her and my father. I wish she hadn't told us. I don't want to know that she's a mom; all of a sudden I can't stand it, that Mary, this woman, is a mom, or that her being a mom means the same thing as what my mom is. I want her to be so different that how she lives could somehow be OK, but how can it be OK? It can't.

She smiles at me and says, "You are traveling with your father?"

I shake my head yes, but can't find words. The connections I have to where I am standing—the same words to name things, the latrine at summer camp, my playhouse in the woods—don't connect me at all, to anything.

"What do you think?" my father whispers to me as we walk back to the van.

He makes whatever is inside me catch fire. I hate everything. And I feel ashamed, which, for all I know, is why my father brought me here—Mr. Expense Account himself, who *made* me try summer camp. I don't know about being poor, or what to say about it, or what to do about it. I'm not Laura. If I were them I'd hate us. How could they not? Hate? But Mr. Otambo doesn't seem to, or even Mary. Do I hate them because of what happened to Laura? I hate the headache I am getting, and my father, and this whole stupid trip.

What do I think?

"I think Mary should get some heated towel racks," I tell him. "I think Mary is a lesbian."

We climb back into the van and I slide to the far end of the seat and fold my arms tight across my chest to stifle my shaking. I have clearly shoved Dad away hard enough this time, because I can feel him not following me anymore, not even standing on the threshold, exasperated. He is gone. He continues the tour with Mr. Otambo, and without me.

He probably thinks I want to be like this—how I'm acting, the words that come slicing out of my mouth, the sound of my voice. Can he really not know that I hate it, too? That I hate everything? *No* one wants to be like this, like no one wants to live like Mary. But it's the way things *are*, what *is* for right now, because of everything that came before, everything that happened whether we wanted it to or not. It's what we've *got*.

Mr. Otambo tells us that the tour is coming to an end, except for a very important part—payment! And then he laughs his hearty laugh.

My father and I do not speak again, really, until our last night in Johannesburg, when he takes me out to dinner at a restaurant recommended by some business friend of his. We are driven there in one of the hotel vans, of course. The city, at least the part where we are, is unbelievably deserted: nobody on the streets, no cars, no people. It's creepy. Dad and I look out the windows of the van and don't say a word.

I feel like we are being freed from a vault when we

finally get to the restaurant and our driver pulls back the van door to let us out. He's being hyper-alert, like a smart dog or cat, darting around, herding us toward the restaurant. My father is walking closer to me than he needs to, than he normally would, and we are following our driver up to the entrance of the restaurant, and we're all kind of scurrying, like we're trying to keep ahead of something dangerous that might be gaining on us but that we can't see or hear behind us. Our driver escorts us right into the restaurant, and as soon as we step inside there is a little breeze of relief as if we *made* it! To where, for what? Everyone covers everything over with thanking our driver for bringing us, and with his thanking us for thanking him, and the restaurant people welcoming us to their empty restaurant.

Our menus are big and filled with choices. I don't feel like eating anymore, but our waiter arrives at the table all friendly and enthusiastic, as if he's genuinely happy to see us and tell us about the food, all the different fishes. His name is Phillip and he is from the Xhosa tribe. He introduces himself in his native language and it is filled up with wonderful clicking sounds. He gets us to try and repeat a word. When we do, he throws back his head and laughs.

I can't help smiling in return. It's like when I was little and had tantrums and my father would tease me out of them before I was ready, make me smile or laugh even though I tried so hard not to let go of being mad. Sometimes I'd start to laugh and it would turn into crying all over again. It's hard for me to go from being so mad to not.

And as soon as our waiter leaves to put in our order, appliance-sized silence comes and sits on the table between my father and me, and we sit there with it until Phillip returns. This time he talks about all the different tribes in South Africa and how Nelson Mandela greeted people in thirteen different languages in his inauguration speech. Phillip tells us that Mandela has eaten at this restaurant twice, and that when he came back the second time he remembered Phillip's name. Phillip talks about him like he loves him, not like he's a politician. He comes right out and says, "Mandela is a very great man. He is like my father." I love what he says and how he says it, but it embarrasses me.

Still, I want Phillip to keep talking, pull up a chair and talk all night. Forget the food. We would pay him, or my father would, to stay with us. Because every time he's with us, telling us stories about where he grew up and his family, it feels good and right and like we are having this special trip, the way it was meant to be, and every time he goes away, to get the food or bring more water or another drink for Dad, it's like the sun goes under a cloud. The sun keeps going in and out the whole night.

Of course Dad wants Phillip to talk about politics, how South Africa has changed now that apartheid is over and Mandela is president. There is so much for me to *learn*, such a golden opportunity! At least Phillip answers with stories so it doesn't get boring. Dad has asked him how the change in government has changed his life.

"Oh," he tells us, "there were a great many terrible things that happened, before."

He is serving us our salads, little mounds of the greenest, freshest baby leaves. He asks us if we want ground pepper, holds up a mill almost as big as a baseball bat. As he's grinding over my father's salad, my father urges him to continue. "Were you involved in the struggle?" he asks.

Phillip laughs. "Oh yes," he says. "*Everyone* was involved in the struggle, whether they knew it or not! The struggle was bigger than all of us. You can hear for yourself—on the radio, still, all the stories. They never end." He is holding the pepper mill steady and straight in his hands. Then he sets it down on a table, next to pitchers of ice water with lemon slices floating on top.

I don't know what he means about the radio. Songs? Some sort of oral-history thing?

"So we know even more now," he says. "The things that were done. But I am not listening anymore on the radio, because I already know what they are talking about, *here,*" and he thumps on his chest, over his heart, like he is knocking on his own front door.

Then he stops knocking and presses both his hands over his heart. "I lost my brothers," he says.

"Brothers?" I say, out loud. I don't mean to, to make him say more, but the word slips out before I can catch it.

"Yes, my brothers." He nods. "One of my brothers was shot down and thrown in a pit," he says, "and another was tortured very badly, so that now he is not speaking, or walking anymore." He stops nodding and shakes his head no.

I want to jump in or jump up and say, "Oh, me *too. My sister* was killed." It sounds crazy, but it's as if I have discovered that Phillip and I are *related* and I want to throw my arms around him. I don't say another word, I don't move.

"We have seen how they tortured him," Phillip is saying, "the bag they put over his head to make him talk. The man who tortured my brother showed us how he pulled the string tighter."

I can't believe what I am hearing, or that I am hearing it here and now, in a fancy restaurant. But I want to hear more, want to know exactly what Phillip is talking about—the bag, the man who pulled the string tighter. I want to see it, too. My hands are dancing in my lap, and then I hear my father say, "I'm so sorry," and I flinch. The sound of his voice—a ragged croak—hangs in the air, unbearably sad. I almost never hear his voice that way, making such a true sound.

"It *is* very sad," Phillip says, nodding again, *"but!"* and his smile returns, flashes: "We have a new country now, a new chance, and I am telling you, we can really *do* something, man!"

I feel my father swoop down out of nowhere to pick up on Phillip's words and run with them. He is going to make a banner out of them that he can drag along behind him as he flies away again. Oh yes, talk about *that*. Tell us how much better things are, let's share our high, high hopes. And Phillip goes! He goes with him!

What about your brothers! I want to scream. What about *Laura*? Wait a minute, we aren't done yet. But *they* are—my father and Phillip are—they have moved on. I see their mouths moving: Phillip is talking, now my father is. They are both going on, together, they are up there in their good-news plane and I am standing down here on the ground, I am probably the smallest speck to them. And as suddenly as I felt related to Phillip, I don't feel related anymore, to anyone or anything—Phillip, my father, the conversation. Whatever leapt up inside me is now crashing its way down through me, to the place where Laura's murder and every other thing I can't stand lives.

For the rest of the meal, they go on and I stay back, with the dead brothers and sister, with a bag that got tightened and somehow Phillip got to see. Every single thing I don't know and can't stand is awake inside me now. I hate it all.

"You got awfully quiet," my father says in the van on the way home.

I am still trying to get everything that got unsprung inside me contained. I give a tight shrug.

"Phillip is an impressive human being," he tries again.

The last thing I want to do is talk to my father. Talking to him never helps. But I cannot make what's inside me stay put, and the things that are hanging out are live wires. I feel wild, electric. "How could Phillip get to see how they tortured his brother?" I blurt out.

My father is surprised by my question. "I assume through the TRC—the Truth and Reconciliation Commission hearings," he says. He pauses to let me remember all the things he has probably told me about it. I remember nothing. "People applying for amnesty acknowledged crimes they had committed under apartheid. Victims and families were able to face their attackers, see who was behind the kidnappings and torture and murders, hear people say what they had done."

"What," I say, "everyone *confessed* to each other? Admitted all the bad stuff they did?" Right!

"Anyone who wanted a chance at amnesty," my father tells me.

"So the man who tortured Phillip's brother admitted what he did—*showed* how he did it, with the bag and the string—in front of everyone?" I am saying it out loud to make sure that I have it straight. My words are gasoline dripping right into my stomach. "They say what they did": the final drip, what it is. And the simple thing it is jolts me. "They say it out loud, in front of everyone. What happened, what they did."

"Yes," my father says, clearly perplexed by my sudden intense interest. "The hearings are still going on, I think. Some of them are broadcast. That's what Phillip meant about listening to the radio." But I am not listening to my father anymore. I am imagining the shadow-men who robbed and killed Laura stepping into the light, showing me how they lifted the rock and brought it down on her head, smashing her skull, showing me the real, human hands that did it, and I feel like I will burst.

I turn and look at my father, crazy with how Laura has risen up inside me, her murder, everything that had finally quieted down, that was *dead*, and is all of a sudden so awake and terrible. And I can't believe how much I want! I want to see who did it, and have them show me what they did, how they hit her—*after* they told her to give them all her money, or before? And what she said to them, would they remember, do murderers *have* memories, how could they stand to? Would they actually say her words, tell if she asked them, please, not to hurt her? Could they open their mouths and tell me, she said *please*? She begged us, but we hit her anyway, we took her money and we left her with her head cracked open, bleeding all over the street? I put my hand over my mouth to try and stop all the words that I am hearing in my head, the outpouring I can't stand and that I want more than anything to actually hear, from them, the ones who did it, *those responsible*. I want at least what Phillip got, and I can't have it, I'll never have it. They got away. The men who killed her got away.

"Berry?" my father says. His voice comes out of

nowhere. I forgot he was here, what we were talking about. We are traveling back to the hotel along a highway whose lights pulse into the van and across my father's face and then leave us momentarily in the dark.

"What's going on in there?" he says, and he taps the top of my head, like me asking Josh, *What're you thinking?* and him always telling me, *Nothing.*

"Nothing," I say. And I shift away from him and look out at the highway. But nothing inside me is quieting down, and it's almost like I can't stop myself from saying something, from getting into this with my father even though I really, really don't want to.

"So if Laura's murderers had been caught," I say, "could they have applied, asked for amnesty, if they were willing to say what they did?"

"No!" my father says, startled, surprised probably by how wrong I've got it, how much I don't understand. "That's not how the TRC works," he says. Now he will tell me how it *does* work, I can feel him gearing up to explain what I do not want to know, or hear. I want people to admit what they did. I want it more than anything.

"The TRC deals with crimes committed under apartheid, for political reasons," my father says. "Not what has happened since apartheid ended, and not with ordinary criminals."

"*Ordinary* criminals killed Laura," I repeat, and it sounds disgusting to me, as if her murder doesn't qualify, isn't good enough. But I am savoring the words— *kill* and *murder* and *criminal*—and I need to keep saying them, now that I've started. There is something about saying them out loud that feels like eating and I've been hungry. I've been starving.

My father pauses, then nods and says, "Right," but I can tell he doesn't know where I'm going with this. Neither do I. But I keep going.

"If they *could*," I say, "if they had caught the murderers and they could apply for amnesty, what would you do? You would want to see them and hear them say what they did. Right?" I make it sound like a despicable thing to want. I am hitting my father with my words now. I feel that, but can't stop, don't want to stop. We are zooming along in the night, moving in and out of pulsing light and dark.

My father shifts uncomfortably. "Berry," he says, like he is cautioning me to slow down a little. "The commission—" he starts, but I interrupt.

"Would you?" I say. I know he wants to keep telling me about how the commission functions, but I won't let him.

"Hypothetical questions are rarely revealing," he says.

"Try a hypothetical answer," I say, skating fast. I am not sure what we are talking about. But I want to stay right where we are: at Laura's murder, saying what happened, saying all the ugly words out loud.

My father sighs. "What you're asking for is full disclosure," he says. "That's what the TRC demands."

"Laura, Dad. *Laura.* Her murder. Her murderers. Do you want to see them, do you want to hold the rock they hit her with?" I am leaning in toward him and I know that Laura was his child and that I am clubbing him, but I cannot not say these words and my voice is low and terrible.

He finally joins me where I am, close to things. I can almost feel him come over. And his voice changes when he says to me, "If you're asking me would it make a difference to see Laura's murderers, to hear them *acknowledge* what they did? Would *that* help? Yes, I think it would. Yes."

We sit, next to each other. My father is with me, wanting to know. It's terrible, but it's where we are and even where I want to be. In a pulse of street light I see his round, fleshy face, not set, not in charge, and right this moment it is enough.

But not for my father. He continues. "And if you're asking, could I forgive them?"—and I gasp because I was *not* asking that, had not considered that: *forgiveness?*—but my father is going on anyway. "Reconciliation is hardly what you would call an operating principle in our culture," he starts off.

I don't want him to say more or go farther, but he does.

"I'd like to think I could come around to it," he says. "But I'd need to become a better man first."

I groan—a low, deep hit of sound. I hate what he has said, how good and noble it is. And what can I possibly say to forgiveness, to needing to be a better man? Everything that's left inside me feels sprung, now, the whole jack-in-the-box, a big mess of busted parts.

We are silent, the van is zooming along, and the air inside it feels heavy with all the stuff we have put out into it. We turn up the winding driveway into the hotel complex. I have to tighten my body so that it doesn't lean into my father as we climb the hill, making turns. It's not until we've stopped and the driver has hopped out to open the door for us that I realize we have not been alone. The driver, this stranger, this black South African man, has heard everything. A wave of embarrassment breaks inside me. Why, though—did I say something so bad, what was the worst thing? The worst thing is having been witnessed this way: raw.

As I step down out of the van, I steal a quick glance at him. His face shows nothing at all, nothing of what he thinks of me or my father or what he overheard. Maybe he hears stuff like this all the time—like Phillip talking about torture. Maybe it's nothing new to him, not in this country of his. Or maybe he's like Josh and he doesn't think anything at all. Why do I even care what he thinks, what Josh thinks, what anyone thinks? He is wearing that ridiculous blue hat with the strap under his chin. How much, how *much* he must hate it! I hear my father tell him good night and thank you, like whatever happened in the van didn't happen.

I walk fast, ahead of my father, and then have to wait at the door for him to come with the key. Once we're inside our suite, I tell myself to go in my room and climb into bed and get to sleep. But I can't make myself do it—go into the bedroom and close the door behind me. I stand in the doorway instead.

My father takes off his shoes in his room, then comes out to the sitting room. He flicks the switch to make the TV rise up out of the floor. I feel some of the springs inside me start to coil—the ones I thought were all broken.

He thinks we are done. We are not done.

I snort at the ascending television set, and when he looks to see what I've snorted at, I say to him, "So is it working *here*, in South Africa? The truth and reconciliation thing?"

"Jury's still out," he says. He walks over to the couch where he'd been hoping to sit and watch TV. "Reconciliation appears to be a slow process."

He is holding the remote control for the TV. If he presses a button I will go over and take it out of his hand and beat him with it. Because I will not, *will not*, go away again from what happened to Laura, and how much I want to know, and what it means. "Do you think they're really sorry for what they did, or do they admit stuff so they can go free?"

What do you want from me? is written all over his face, his big, round, lined face. He sighs. "I don't know, Berry," he says, pressing back against the couch. "I can't speak for them." He looks at me. It is not the way he looked at Laura in the car that night, when they had their important political discussion. He is not loving this, talking to me.

"Well, what would *you* do?" I ask. "Would you say what *you* did—the worst, the cruelest thing? And then ask to go free?"

He looks confused.

I don't mind elaborating, saying more. I like whatever it is I've stumbled into. "I mean, if you thought you could get away with the worst thing you ever did? If you were willing to admit it? Would you show how you *tortured* someone?"

I am desperate to have him answer me, and I am ready to hate however he answers. I am poised, rock in hand.

He looks at me, pained. "Berry," he says, "I don't know what it is you're asking me." He leans in toward me and says, very slowly, "I am not the criminal." He moves his head back and forth as he practically whispers, "I didn't murder anyone."

I feel the rock in my hand but I cannot throw it at him, cannot even lift it. I feel myself shrinking inside the doorway. "I didn't say you were," I manage, finally, to say. I sound five.

The silence between us is awful, and my father tries to fill it. He offers a bigger fact, something to move us away from Laura, or him and me, or whatever it is we are talking about. "Remorse was not required by the commission. They asked for full disclosure and acknowledgment—that's what they consider the key to moving forward."

"Wait a minute," I say, as his words sink in. "The

people who did the bad things don't have to be *sorry* for what they did?" Everything in me throbs. "Of *course* they have to be," I say. "God. *God!*"

He looks at me but doesn't answer, frustrated that he has set me off again.

"Dad," I say, demanding. "People *have* to be sorry for hurting other people. They have to be!"

We have a moment where we simply look at each other and in that moment my demand crystallizes inside me: *Be sorry. You* be sorry. I want that more than anything, and I want *him* to give it to me. *You* be sorry, Dad.

My father is clenching against whatever place we've come to. He looks like he is about to bolt off the couch, a football player ready to move down the field, fast. He doesn't know what to do, or what to say to me. I can feel how much he wants to get away from all this—from me and everything that I am asking. It hits me then: I know *exactly* how he feels. He could swim a thousand laps about now. And if I weren't part of the everything he wanted to go away from, I'd be all for it, wave good-bye, go myself.

He has put down the clicker, folded his thick, wide hands together, settled his elbows onto his knees, and he is leaning forward so that his head and his clasped hands and his feet are all in line. The sight of him like that—bowed—kills me. He looks like he could be praying. I hold my breath. I wait for him to raise his head and look at me and tell me he is sorry.

He raises his head and looks at me. "Enough, Berry," he says. "I think we've had enough for one night. I'm going to bed."

I WAKE UP WITH EVERYTHING FROM last night still inside me. I have not even opened my eyes, but I am seeing my father with his head bent and his hands together, leaning forward on the couch, looking sorry. I am seeing him that way when he gives a fast knock on my door and startles me.

"Berry? Time to get up."

When I don't answer back right away, he cracks the door open and pokes his head in. "Berry," he says again, this time more serious, more of a statement. "Up and at 'em." He reminds me that our plane to Kruger Park leaves at seven-thirty. "OK?" he says. "Are you with me?"

"All *right,*" I say, with more of a snap than I meant to, but he is so over-eager, so primed, so not on the couch with his head bowed down. I can feel him practically vibrating with what's coming up—three days with the wild animals at some national park. Like last night never happened, like we didn't talk about the things we did. He has already moved on, past it all, to the future, and I haven't started on today.

We pack in our separate rooms, Dad calling out reminders and suggestions as they come to him. Did I bring enough film? I could put together a slide show for school, he tells me, do a mixed-media presentation about Kruger. Dad just can't get enough of projects. I remember endlessly studying the rain forest in fourth and fifth grade, weeks of turning our classroom into a crepe paper jungle. By the end I *wanted* the rain forest wiped out so we could shut up about it.

After a few of his suggestions that I don't respond to he's back at my door.

"Berry," he says, "I went to a lot of trouble to put this part of the package together."

"I know that," I answer him, evenly. What a stupid word: *package*.

"I want you to get the most out of it."

I know that too. Obviously. Who *doesn't* want to get the most out of what they do? But who decides what *most* is? Or *enough*? Obviously my father does. How silly of me to forget that, even for a second.

"If that's not too much to ask," he finishes.

His words go through my back—which is turned to him—and land in my stomach, and then they make my eyelids heavy. It's a weird back-stomach-eye connection. "Why would it be too much to ask?" I say, and I snap the shorts I am holding out in front of me, and then I lay them on the bed and fold them over and smooth them out and fold them again and put them in my backpack. He stands still in my doorway for a second more and doesn't say anything, and then he goes back to his room.

Lions and tigers and bears, I whisper. Lions and tigers and bears.

The drive to Kruger is several hours from the tiny airport where we land. I sleep—or pretend to—nearly the whole way. When I was little I faked being asleep so I could listen to Mom and Dad talk about things they wouldn't if they thought I was awake.

I also played blind a lot, with Laura. She gave me the longest turns at being the one who was blind, made sure I didn't walk into telephone poles or mailboxes or step out into the street. She always called out if something was dangerous. It was my favorite game.

My eyes are closed now, but I can feel how much my father wants me to be awake and alert, like how I know when Josh wants to fool around even if he's not touching me.

Dad keeps announcing things as if I *were* awake, or cared, or we had been talking away with each other the whole time. "Twenty kilometers more," he says. "We're getting there."

Right.

"Crocodile Bridge," he announces at our entry point to the park. I almost sit up and look out, it's hard not to, having heard the word *crocodile*. Behind my eyelids I see a ticking cartoon creature and Captain Hook running so fast across the water that his legs look like a circular saw. I manage to stay still and keep my eyes closed, but I feel a little grin widen my mouth. I loved *Peter Pan*. I must have watched it a million times when I was a kid. And Laura could do the most perfect imitation of Captain Hook's voice, his wicked laugh, his demand for a *tarantella*!

So I am off in never-never land when Dad pulls over and announces that he is going to register and get directions to our campsite. When he comes back he leans in to me and says, "Wake up, Berry, I need you to read the map."

"I bet," I say—it pops out of me, because it's obvious that he's pissed, and because he startled me. But it is

kind of rude to wake me up—I know I *looked* asleep—
and how hard can it be to follow a road map inside a
park?

"Excuse me?" he says. "Pardon me?"

"Forget it," I say, and reach over and take the map
and pretend to read it. I don't have a clue where we are,
or where we're headed.

"Am I asking too much?" he says. "Imposing? Inter-
rupting your busy schedule?"

"Sorry," I say, but I'm not, that much is clear. All I
know is that we are back to our crummy way of being
with each other.

"I think maybe we need to get some things straight
before we go too much farther," he says. We are driving
down the one road there is, the only car on it. I fold my
arms across my chest and sigh.

My attitude, for one thing. My ingratitude. I tune in,
tune out, tick tock, Captain Hook buzzing across the water. Now and then I catch a word—*responsibility* or *effort*,
nothing as good as *crocodile*—and then long stretches of
nothing but background noise. I think we're like that
cartoon where all the dog hears the master saying is blah
blah blah.

All of a sudden I realize that I am looking at giraffes,
long and knobby-kneed, right *next* to our car, practically,

nibbling the trees that line the road. I actually gasp, and Dad brakes and stops talking mid-sentence and we both stare, amazed. I guess I wasn't ready for them not to be in cages, not even hiding. And here they are, beside us, so close I can see the way their lips wiggle when they chew. And how long their eyelashes are, so long they look fake.

"Well," Dad says, when he finally drives on, "that was a surprise."

Oh, Fred, look at that tree, I almost say back to him—what we used to say about Washington tourists at cherry blossom time, a line that used to be a family joke, when we used to be a family. I don't say it, though, don't see how it could possibly survive the trip from way back then to here and now.

Dad is resuming his lecture, anyway. "I think it's important," he starts, and his words make the air in the car feel heavy. Before he can even finish his opening thought, though, we both see wart hogs, a batch of them, to our right, rooting around in the grass. They all have tusks, even the fat little babies. We watch them scuffle around, wart hogs of every size, digging for something in the earth. Dad's unfinished sentence hangs in the air, and I settle in to watch, but after a while Dad slowly pulls forward again.

"That was a surprise," I say, the way he did. He looks at me to see if I am mocking him, or serious. I am seriously mocking him, but he lets it pass. I wonder if he'll return to the point he was trying to make, give it one more shot. And then, before he can, in front of us and larger than life: zebras, a whole herd of them, a mass of beautiful, perfect stripes. Dad edges the car closer and then brakes, and we finally both give ourselves over to sitting and staring, all out. It's clear that at least for now the lecture is over. He has finally lost, and to animals!

We watch the zebras for a while, and for the first time since I woke up this morning I start to feel not totally caught in quicksand, and like maybe I won't have to sleep the whole trip no matter what.

Our cabin is a circular hut with a thatched roof—one of about twelve or fifteen that dot the compound. It has two twin beds and a little bathroom with a shower. It has everything we need, and no more. I don't say out loud how much I like it, but I really do. I take some clothes out of my backpack and hang them on the pegs. I like pegs.

Dad says he could use a rest. Now that I finally feel better, he clearly feels worse. It's like we're on some kind of awful seesaw. I leave him and sit outside on the small front porch. Birds with beaks like bruised bananas are scrounging around the yard. When I look out in the distance, way beyond the fence that encircles the compound, I see the perfect silhouette of three elephants walking single file along the horizon. Strange umbrella-topped trees look like punctuation on the flat line of land. It takes a second to dawn on me that what I'm seeing is real—real animals just walking along where they live, moving slowly and steadily forward.

I feel bad about how I acted this morning.

I'm not dumb; I know this whole trip is metaphor city—everyone everywhere trying to forgive each other and get on with it: South Africans, us about Laura, Dad and me. I get it, I just don't get how.

About twenty people from our little cluster of cabins show up for the night ride through the park, and we sit in rows of four or five in an open-topped, oversize Jeep. Our driver, one of the park rangers, has handed out a few flashlights so that once the sun goes down we can use them to catch the eyes of animals that come out at night to hunt.

There's a real *family* sitting in the row in front of Dad and me—a mom and dad and their two good-looking sons and a girlfriend of one of the sons. They have all squinched in together in the second row, and they've brought a picnic basket with wine and beer and snacks. They seem to know exactly what they are doing and why they are here. They act rich. They jabber away, the brothers tease each other back and forth, almost like they have their own separate language. I stare at them and listen to everything they say. I am so interested! Josh wouldn't be, he'd call them happy assholes.

My father leans forward, gets closer to the happy family. Of course he has to talk to them, interview them, pretend that we're in this together. He can never just look.

The next thing I know we're all saying our names to each other and smiling. The sons barely look at me when they say hello, and the girlfriend isn't interested, either—it's so obvious they have everything they need with each other, it's not like they're looking to bring anyone else inside their circle—but the adults glom on to each other right away, ready to talk and act like best friends.

They are the Andersons, this happy family, and they have been doing this all their lives, coming to the park for vacations and long weekends, since the boys were very little, going out on night drives and spotting the biggest animals—elephants, leopards, lions, rhinoceroses. One of the sons, Robert, pops the top of a beer can and passes it to his brother. They could be swimmers, these guys, at least lifeguards. They have the right bodies, and all the confidence in the world.

The ranger has started up the Jeep and is pulling out of the campsite compound, heading toward a watering hole where the animals come to drink at night. The sun has not gone down yet, but it is setting and the light is beautiful and the air is cool. I give myself a little reality check: I am in South Africa. With my father. We are on the lookout for wild animals.

Now the Andersons have offered my father some wine in a plastic cup they've pulled out of their picnic basket. He thanks them very much. I say no to a soda. Their comfort with themselves, with being here on the night ride, with each other, explaining the whole South African park system to my father—it kind of takes over the whole bus. Everyone else is quiet and shy, and this row of happy family more or less *reigns* over the rest of us.

Maybe my family was like that, a long time ago: a reigning happy family. Definitely when Laura was in high school and winning every award there was to win, and Mom and Dad and I were always there, together, applauding. And vacations, too—we must have looked good then, probably even happy, on our camping trips in Virginia, on our trips to the Eastern Shore. It's so funny to think of that, now, and here, in South Africa—spying on this perfect-looking family and thinking I could ever have been in their place, or that someone could have sat behind me and seen me that way.

The girlfriend is leaning into Robert. Her hair is shiny and black, pulled into a ponytail. Her skin is perfect. Every once in a while they give each other a little kiss. They're not exactly keeping their eyes peeled for animals, either. So far it's only been bok, which look like deer. Her silky ponytail bobs back and forth when she talks and laughs. I think about leaning forward and yanking it.

Robert says something I can't catch and then gives his brother a quick punch on his biceps. He has probably thrown the same punch a thousand times, moved his head back at the exact angle, smiled broadly with his big, bright, perfect teeth. But something in the way the other brother lowers his head and tightens his mouth lets me see how much he hates being hit, hates how Robert does that to him. I am relieved to see it. I can't stand thinking that *nothing* bad has ever happened to these people.

It's almost like I *hope* Robert has beat on his brother all their lives. Or that the mom and dad can't stand each other, or there used to be a daughter. Who died. Just to make them not so perfect, so happy, so pleased with themselves and sitting up there in front of my father and me.

Even if someone in the Anderson family hasn't died, someone will, eventually. That's weird: feeling relieved to know that sooner or later *everyone* dies, and everything can change in an instant, even in the happiest families.

So now I'm looking at them and I'm not sure who they are, which makes it harder to hate them. But not hating them doesn't feel great, either.

It's dark now—a darkness that came so gradually I didn't notice until it was over us. The night air has turned chilly and we've pulled out the wool blankets from under our seats and spread them across our laps. Robert is manning the flashlight and he does a good job of shining it into the night. A guy in the back of the Jeep jiggles his all over and it gives me a headache to try and follow his beam. Robert holds the light low and steady and he catches a lot of eyes, so far small stuff.

Suddenly Robert yells out, "Stop!" and everyone

shushes him because he said it so loud—the ranger warned us not to make sudden noises. But there is a lion—a lion!—lying right on the side of the road, a few feet away.

I spot it at almost the same moment as Robert; my father is still shifting in his seat to see what's there. The instant he does see it, he grabs my hand. He startles me, and I can't help it: I flinch, my hand jumps back, out of his, like it got burned or touched by some monster that came out of the dark to get me. And as soon as I flinch, *he* flinches, a little jolt in his body that I register in mine, all this happening in such a fraction of a second: our silent, jumpy conversation—so rapidly begun and concluded—and the lion in the road has tensed at being in the spotlight.

The people holding the lights skim the land around and behind him and find the family, the mother and cubs, about ten yards back, clustered together and gnawing the toppled carcass of a giraffe. One of the cubs is actually *inside* the ripped-open rib cage of the giraffe and chewing on it from the inside out. The sight amazes me and all I want is to be here seeing it, but I feel my hands, cold, on my lap, and this awful weight about what just happened between my father and me that I didn't even *mean* to have happen. I steal a quick look at him and he's staring like mad at the lions. But my having pulled away from him is inside how hard he is staring. I turn back to the lions eating, the splayed legs of the giraffe and the skeleton of its ribs. With all the lights trained on them, everything is illuminated, even smears of blood on the cubs' mouths, like they forgot to wipe! All I want is to watch them and for there to be nothing else. I fold my hands together and squeeze, as if that will make whatever is extra—and hurting—go away.

Soon hyenas appear on the scene, but they keep a respectful distance from the eating lions. Eventually they make their way toward our vehicle and begin to circle it. Their heads seem too small for their bodies, and not fully formed: they look like they have missing bones. I look at my father again, I nod and smile so that he will know I think this is cool, that I am glad to be here seeing it, that I didn't mean to jerk my hand away, but I don't know if it's too late or not.

Our driver, the ranger, quietly tells us that the hyenas are waiting for the lions to finish up so that they can scavenge whatever is left. They hunt for themselves, too, she tells us, and are such ferocious fighters that some pups start fighting with each other when they're still in the amniotic sac, before they are fully born.

Two of the hyena pups have roamed over to my side

of the Jeep and are taking swipes at each other, beginning to tussle like puppies or cats, or like Robert and his brother, throwing little punches at each other. One of the bigger ones comes along behind them and nudges them forward and apart. Probably their mother. Or father.

We watch for a long time, and a deep quiet settles over everyone. No one gets bored, being feet away from lions and hyenas. I'm still holding my hands together pretty tightly. My ache isn't any worse than it was. I can't help what happened, and it's over—that's what I tell myself when it starts to come up inside me again. I imagine myself saying to my father that I didn't mean to pull away, that he startled me. How hard could that be, to tell him, casually, when we get to the campsite, when we're climbing off the bus?

I go back to watching the feeding lions, and the one in the road who is so in charge, and the waiting, roaming hyenas. I really do forget about everything else, and when the ranger says it's about time to return to camp and we finally pull away, I can feel how satisfied everyone on the bus is, like *we're* the ones who had the good meal.

As we are climbing out of the Jeep at the compound, Mr. and Mrs. Anderson invite us back to their cabin. My insides clench. I want to stay with what I've seen, the animals, how quiet everyone got. I don't want to go somewhere else. Then I look at my father and I can see how much he wants to have a drink and talk with these people he doesn't even know.

I say I'm kind of tired, tell Dad to go ahead. The brothers and the girlfriend have already headed off. "Really," I emphasize to my father, because he has that slightly torn look he sometimes gets before he does what he wants to anyway.

I walk as far as the Andersons' cabin with them, and Mrs. Anderson says again that she'd love to have me visit for a while, but I beg off and head for Dad's and my cabin without looking at him or answering back when he calls out good night. I remember that I was going to tell Dad I was sorry I yanked my hand away. But the Andersons beat me to him, and of course he wanted to go. I step up onto the little porch of our hut. I'd *wanted* to be nice, and now, instead, I'm being meaner!

I stand in front of the door, key in hand. I freeze, all of a sudden, the way I sometimes do letting myself in at home, after school. But I can't go over to Mom's office, drop in on her and Leroy. It's not the same at all: I'm on the other side of the world, standing in front of a whole different door. Josh isn't breathing down my neck behind me. And I know where Dad is, even if I don't want to be there with him.

I make myself turn the key in the lock and when I push open the door I see my soft blue sweatshirt and my shorts hanging on the pegs. It's a little thing—seeing my own stuff—but it makes me feel better about being here by myself. I'm *not* scared! Especially not of the animals.

I leave the light on, though, when I climb into bed. That way Dad won't have to fumble around when he comes back. I picture Dad over in the Andersons' cabin, drink in hand, talking. I think of Mom back at home, probably in the kitchen, or in the living room watching TV. Lying on my narrow bed, I edge toward sleep, remember the giraffe's rib cage with the cub inside it, and the lions with blood on their mouths, and the crazed-looking hyenas who are still a family anyway.

In the morning Dad wakes me up out of a dream. I think it was a swimming dream; I have that watery feeling around me. It's really early, six or something. I want to tell him that the animals aren't going anywhere, that we have the whole day to drive around and look at them. And weren't we were out spotting them a few hours ago, in the dark? But I don't say anything. I get up and eat a banana and get in the car when he tells me to. As soon as I've buckled my seat belt, though, I lean my head against the window and start to doze right away because I am really, truly sleepy.

And I am really, truly asleep when Dad brakes so sharply that my head snaps forward and I push against my seat belt as I jolt awake. "What?" I say, instantly scared, instantly mad. "What?"

"Look," he says. "There."

I look around and don't see anything. Just a huge pile of steaming crap in the middle of the road. I turn to my father. "You woke me up to see *that*?" I ask.

"Yes," he tells me. "Dung. Or, as it's commonly called," he says, looking right at me, "shit." He raises his eyebrows up. "Shit, Berry. I thought you might be interested to see a pile of what you seem to think the whole world is full of."

Is he *crazy*? He's actually scaring me a little, I feel it on the back of my neck.

"Nothing else seems to interest you," he says evenly. "I thought this might." He turns to look out at the pile in the road again, as if he is watching TV. I hold still. My heart is hammering, I feel like I have to *tiptoe*, that things are fragile.

"Am I wrong?" he continues, still watching the

steaming pile in the road. "Mistaken in thinking that you find this world and most of what's in it barely worth opening your eyes to take in? A veritable *crock*?" A little smile flits across his face. It's awful.

I don't know what to do. I look at the shit in the road, too—this enormous dump. I don't do anything.

And after a little while of holding perfectly still, not getting it, I get it: it's because I pulled my hand away. Or wouldn't go over to the Andersons'. It's because I haven't told him that anything we're seeing interests me. He's mad at me and now he's acting like a jerk, he's acting like a *baby*.

At least knowing stops me from being scared. Why be scared of a baby? I turn and look at the pile and sit, like he is, watching it. I actually kind of settle in. I can do this, too, for as long as he can. Maybe longer.

But after a while it's too weird, this stupid game we're both playing. "What was it?" I ask, to break it up.

He obviously doesn't get what I mean.

"What *left* it?" I say.

"Oh," he says. "An elephant. There were three."

I look out across the empty land we can see in front of and around us. I remember the silhouettes of the elephants I saw at the campsite yesterday, their loping forward progress across the horizon. A sad *oh* comes out of me and I tell my father, "I'm sorry I missed them."

What I say makes a difference I can see on his face. He comes back a little from how set against me he was. He releases some air out of his anger, like those balloons that slowly deflate. And the release opens things up between us for a second—we could each make a move toward the other. Seeing the chance is as far as I get before the moment passes and my father takes his foot off the brake and we drive on, around the dung.

We go back to our campsite for lunch at the cafeteria. First we wander through the gift shop looking at tacky postcards and carvings. Then Dad notices there's a display about elephants at the ecology center next door. "Hey, Berry, look," he says. "This might be interesting." I smile, thinking of the pile of shit, but I follow him in.

It's better than a crepe paper rain forest, but there are still too many maps with pushpins and tiny type on cards. Dad has to read every explanation, study every display. I pretty much stay parked in front of an elephant's heart in a jar. Finally he joins me there.

"I never said the whole world was full of shit," I tell him, quietly.

He looks at me for a second, startled, then back at the

display. "It's more of an unspoken attitude that you convey," he says.

I don't respond. I really *don't* think everything is full of shit. Not *everything*!

Dad's voice softens a little bit when he says, "You keep your eyes closed a lot of the time, Berry."

My eyes! My closed eyes! I feel like he has named this intimate part of me. "So?" I say back to him. But my mouth has gone all twisty. I have this awful, I-might-cry feeling. When I speak again, I make sure my chin and lips are tight. "Just because I close my eyes doesn't mean I think everything outside is ... worthless."

My father looks at me; I keep my eyes on the heart in the jar. But I can tell he is not mad anymore. He'd probably rather be—it must be pretty obvious I am trying not to cry, and he doesn't know what to do when people get emotional and he hates not knowing what to do.

"Well, yes," he says. "Not necessarily. It's hard to know *what* it means."

Leroy's name means the king. I don't know what my closed eyes mean. Only that sometimes it feels better to be in the dark, away from everything. But it's not the same as when I played blind and had Laura to call out to me, warning; or her fingers on my back when she taught me to float.

I turn to my father and shrug, don't even try to say anything more.

"I know," he says. "It's tough."

And we stand and look at the heart a little longer. It's absolutely enormous.

Our last day at Kruger is hot and cloudless. We're leaving at one to catch our flight to Cape Town. The sun is high and the road dusty and dry. A few miles before we exit the park we pull into one of the few rest stops where you're allowed to get out of your car. But there are signs all over saying not to feed the monkeys and warning you to watch out for animals. We stand and look down a ravine to the wide stream below. A few other people have stopped, too, real intent with their binoculars. Even without binocs it's easy to see the two hippopotamuses in the water. One is blaring at the other, stomping, making moves but not really closing in. The other one is holding completely still. I'm so sure they're going to fight, but we watch for a long time and it never comes. They keep doing what they're doing—the one blaring and stomping water and the other holding perfectly still.

Finally I come up with a story. I think that the one who isn't moving is mad and keeping it to herself. Pouting. And the loud one is trying to get her attention. And then I realize who it is I'm seeing: George and Martha! *George and Martha*, my favorite book when I was a kid! I *loved* those stories. Mom and Dad used to read them to me all the time, over and over. And *that's* what I think I'm watching down in the water: best friends who are mad at each other, but not really, not for long, not forever. I almost tell Dad, but I don't. I look at him; he's watching the hippos and is obviously pretty caught up in the show. I actually feel my silence sticking to me, clinging, like it has Velcro or something, and I can't open my mouth (rip the Band-Aid off fast, get it over with) and say some simple thing that would connect us. He looks at me, then, and I do: "George and Martha!" I blurt out.

For a second I think he might not remember. But he does, I watch his remembering come into his face. "Exactly!" he says, and we turn back to watch them, together. And now maybe we *both* think that the hippo on the right is wearing a pink tutu and ballet slippers, trying to hold on to being mad at her best friend in the world. It's probably pathetic to put a made-up story on top of what's real, but that's what I've done. And it feels better, at least right this minute, as we're about to leave this place, for Dad and me to be seeing the same thing.

BEING WITH THE ANIMALS—FOR
just a few days—makes being in
Cape Town, in a regular hotel,
feel pretty strange. All we're really doing now is filling up time
until the ceremony. Five more days. Dad has scheduled
sightseeing and a trip to the wine country.

"Berry?" he calls out to me. "Want to say hello to your
mother?"

I didn't know Dad was even talking to Mom. I thought
he was checking on final arrangements for the memorial service. I pick up the extension in my room. "Hello?"

"Darling," she says, "how are you?"

I feel a little shy—maybe the distance between us, or
the surprise of hearing her voice, or that I'm here with
Dad and not there with her.

Right away Dad says, "I'm gonna sign off," and
hangs up.

"Darling," she says again, and we start our conversation for real. "Tell me."

I tell her I'm good. When she asks about Kruger I actually have a lot to say, I launch into things. My own voice surprises me, how chipper I sound. But I know it probably sounds good to Mom, so I go with it.

As I'm telling her about the lions and hyenas I remember my hand jerking away and Dad flinching in response. I don't let it interrupt the story, though. I tell her about the elephants loping by, and the hippopotamuses, not the pile of crap in the road. I like having something to give her.

"How's the king?" I ask her, and she tells me about her kids, all the progress they're making. It's funny to sit and hear her talk about her kids from so far away, me in a hotel room looking out the window at this massive flat-topped mountain that rises up and looms above the whole city. I tell her that Table Mountain is right in front of me, a table set to bear the weight of the world, the *mother* of all tables. And I tell her that Cape Town feels more alive and free than Johannesburg did. At least there are lots of people out and walking around, and we're near the ocean, and it's beautiful. I stop there, with it being beautiful, because we're near where Laura died and closer to the memorial service and I can only go so far.

"How are *you*?" I manage to slip in, when I can feel her getting ready to say good-bye.

There is a pause. "I'm all right," she says. "I am aware of being alone."

"Oh," I say, crushed suddenly. "But you're OK," I say, telling her what I need to hear back.

"I am *definitely* OK," she says, "doing fine and looking forward to having you home."

As soon as we've hung up I feel this awful pang from having heard her voice and knowing she's alone and from everything I *didn't* tell her. I made things sound all one way, all good and fine.

Dad's plan for today is to visit Robben Island, where Nelson Mandela was imprisoned, but now he tells me that first we are going to drive out to the school where the ceremony will be, to make sure everything is all set. Whatever Dad is involved in he has to run, even if it's not his show.

Driving through downtown we pass by places Laura wrote about in her letters home—all her hopeful, excited letters. At the stoplights black men with I DON'T DO CRIME! lettered on the backs of their jackets move among the stopped cars selling things, but everyone has their windows rolled up and their doors locked. The lights change before any of the men get to our car.

We drive outside the city to where things are dry and dusty and have that pulled-down feeling, to where it's poor. When we're sitting in our fancy hotel I like to think poverty is better or more noble, but being in it kind of depresses me. The sun starts to feel mean, there are flies everywhere, and no trees or flowers or one pretty thing. The buildings remind me of the way kids draw houses, the basic box and roof line and a hole for the door and a window, nothing extra, no details. Bunches of black men are hanging around on the corners, in front of bars and gas stations. They have nothing to do and it shows all over them, like having nothing to do has become who they are.

I start to feel in my bones—forget geography or maps—that we are nearer than ever to where Laura got killed. We are getting closer and everything is closing in.

Dad is concentrating hard on finding the school.

"There," he announces when he reads the street sign and sees the buildings up ahead. He sounds relieved.

The church and school are fenced off and a little separate—they haven't been given up on, like most of the places surrounding them. We park and go into the church. It's dark and cool inside—a definite change—but I can still feel the dry, glaring, poor world outside pulsing against its walls. I can't believe Laura *chose* this place to come and be.

The church is empty except for the priest, at the altar, talking to two young boys. He is showing them something, and when he sees us he throws up his arms in greeting and walks down. He is wearing priest clothes—vestments?—and they billow out around him and he rustles as he approaches us. He has a great big smile, like he heard a good joke up there at the altar. I'm so glad to have the dark coolness of the church washing over me, and I'd like to surrender to it, but the man who is walking down the aisle toward us is huge, and so present, that I actually *can't* drift away. Dad marches up to him, hand extended.

The priest takes my father's hand and wraps his other arm around him and folds him into a great big hug! He must not know that people don't do that to my father, but here he is, getting away with it.

"And you are Berry," he says, turning to me. He does not hug me, he studies me. I know this is Father Alan, who Laura wrote about in her letters and I saw in pictures she sent home.

"That's me," I say, because I don't know *what* to say, and I feel funny even talking out loud in a church— shouldn't we be whispering?

But he is talking loudly, and clearly. He welcomes us both and then he asks me, "Where did your name come from? Berry."

"Oh," I answer, and I can feel my face warming from the inside out, "it's a nickname. Because I spent so much time in the pool, and my mother said I turned brown as a berry." I wish my name *meant* something, like Leroy's.

"I see," he says, nodding, as if it's a good thing to know about me, my name, and I'm blushing more now because I am talking to a man whose blackness *shines*, and the idea of me being dark or tan or brown seems so ridiculous here in Africa.

"Laura spoke of you many, many times," he tells me. "She missed you when she was here with us. And now we all miss Laura *terrifically*!" The word dances out of his mouth like he is singing it. He sounds so happy, so enthusiastic—as if he doesn't know Laura has died, as if she has just gone on to some other place. "We had great *fun* together!" he says.

None of what he is saying adds up for me—talking so happily about Laura, saying she was fun, not even whispering.

Father Alan continues studying me, and then he says he does not see Laura in me on the outside—the way I look. "You must keep the things she gave you on the inside," he says, only part question.

What he says is too fast, too intimate—talking about what's inside me—but it's also a relief to be hearing things that matter, even if I don't completely understand. I feel like I haven't had real words with anyone in a long time. It's strange, though, to get them all of a sudden, out of nowhere, from a smiling man in robes in a run-down church. I'd like to join him in being light and kind of brimming, but I don't know how. "I suppose," I say, not much of an answer.

It's weird, then, for a second, with no one saying anything, so of course Dad jumps in and takes charge. He starts asking questions about the ceremony, only they don't sound like questions. He mostly goes over the plan. The plan is for me to present the check for the money raised at the swimathon to Father Alan immediately after the unveiling of the memorial stone. Dad says that perhaps I'll have a few words to say. Every time he goes over the plan with me, he says there will be an opportunity for me to speak if I want to. Who does he think I *am*? Laura? Some Student Council president, the kid who wins the awards and makes the speeches? I'm not talking, I'm not. I feel like I'm filled with stones, a tower of them. They are in my stomach, in my throat, I have pebbles on my tongue. Soon I will not be able to speak at all. *Please don't make me do this* may be the last words I ever say.

I step back, away from my father and Father Alan, and sit down at the very end of one of the pews, my hand clutching its post. My body is heavy as lead. Dad and Father Alan keep talking about the ceremony on Monday. I close my eyes. I do not want to do, or see, anything. I want the next four days to be over, all the sights seen and the wine country visited and the memorial to Laura unveiled. I want to be home, I want to be under water.

In an instant I feel Father Alan's heavy, soft hand cover my own, even as he continues talking to Dad. I open my eyes to see his massive, dark hand weighting mine, resting there until the conversation is over and it is time for us to go.

Glaring light and heat hit Dad and me as we step outside the church. It is an effort to walk my body over to the car and wait while Dad unlocks the doors. As soon as we get in, he reaches for the map and plots our route to the dock where we will catch the Robben Island ferry. "Are you all *right?*" he says to me quickly, telling me exactly what my answer needs to be.

"Yep," I say, and we head off.

The air is so much cooler on the water, and the sun feels good again, baking me; the sky is perfectly blue. I sink into my padded seat on the snappy white boat that is ferrying a whole group of us over to Robben Island. We could all be heading out to some vacation spot off the coast of Maine, a boatload of white tourists with our sunglasses on. But we're going to see a *prison*, where Nelson Mandela spent twenty-five years!

I've never known anyone who went to prison. Dad knows people in Washington who've been indicted, none of them likely to end up sentenced to life with hard labor. And the guys who get in trouble in Washington aren't exactly Nelson Mandela. God, Laura loved him. He was her biggest hero. She wrote about coming here, in one of her letters home. I am trying to remember what she said, but all I remember is the envelope, her round, blue handwriting sprawled out over every inch of the paper, and me lying on my bed, reading it. Robben Island was another place she wrote about—like a movie she had seen but I hadn't.

The tour starts off more like nature study once we're off the ferry. We go around the island by bus before we go inside any of the buildings, and there are small herds of bok out in the fields, in the distance, some of them nibbling at tree branches. Our guide tells us that once there had been a plan to turn the island into a zoo and so they started bringing out animals, but the plan got changed and they decided to cage people here instead. And way before they ever put a prison on it, the island was a leper colony.

A woman with a German accent who is sitting behind me on the bus says to her husband, "Everyone they did not want got sent here." She says *vant*. I lean over and whisper to Dad, "I wonder if she and her husband visit the concentration camps in Germany, or if they only go to bad places in other countries."

Dad looks offended by what I've said. But then he seizes the moment to teach me a thing or two. "Every country has history to be ashamed of," he says. He starts listing chapters of American history that could qualify: annihilating Indian tribes, Salem witch trials, herding Japanese-Americans into internment camps during World War II, lynchings. "Kent State," he says. "I believe there's a memorial where the National Guard gunned down the protesters." I hope he doesn't go off about the '60s. I'm sorry I brought the whole thing up.

"Look!" a man on the bus calls out suddenly, and points to a huge black bird in the sky, circling. The woman in front of us says it is a vulture. I look. But this isn't Kruger, I think. We're here for something else, I don't know what.

Our next stop on the bus tour is the limestone quarry where Mandela and the other prisoners had to work every day breaking rocks. Walls of white limestone spike up toward the sun, like some kind of gleaming, awful castle. Our guide tells us that the prisoners weren't allowed to wear glasses, and a lot of them got eye problems from the glare—some condition that blocked their tear ducts and made it so they couldn't cry. I never knew there was a condition like that. I thought you had to do it to yourself.

As we are leaving the quarry our guide points out a little tower of stones. He tells us that after the prison was shut down Mandela and a bunch of the former prisoners revisited the island. They walked to the quarry where they had spent years of their lives pounding rocks. Before they left, each man picked up a stone and set it down, in memory. That's the tower we're looking at, right out in the open, for everyone to see.

Inside the prison a man named Michael takes over as our tour guide. All the guides are former political prisoners. That really gets me. And it's stupid, but I keep looking at Michael to see if he *looks* like a prisoner, the way I study pictures of murderers in the newspaper to see if they look like murderers. What do I expect, some little pitchfork above their heads, yellow eyes? There is so much that doesn't show on the outside—which was probably Father Alan's point.

But I keep looking at Michael, studying him. And what I see is a strong black man, standing in front of me, willing to show me the place where he was jailed for twenty years of his life.

We make a semicircle around him so everyone can hear what he is saying, and then start to move through the prison section by section. This feels completely different from some stupid class trip, being dragged around the National Gallery by some blabby guide talking about symbolism. Michael points to a narrow staircase and tells us that up there was the most hated room on Robben Island. I think torture, interrogation. I think of what Phillip said about the bag over his brother's head, how he is not walking anymore. I want Michael to say more, like I wanted Phillip to.

"That is the room where the guards read the letters that were sent to us—we could receive one letter a month, twelve letters a year—and they cut out any information they wanted to before they handed them over. Sometimes we would get a letter with only the signature of the person who wrote it." He says what a hard thing it is to have news from the people you love taken away from you. "You have to have *stories*," he says. He says it so fiercely I hold my breath. He shakes his tightened fist as if it holds all the stories that were taken out of all the letters, and then he doesn't say any more. Finally he ushers us along: "Ladies and gentlemen, let us move forward."

I am thinking of Laura's letters, how much she wrote about what she was doing and seeing and how little most of it mattered to me. It was all too big—Africa, politics, revolution. *History* is too big! I liked her stories about dancing and going out with friends, wanted her to say when she was coming home and what we'd do after she got back.

But the last letter she wrote I read over and over and over, as if every word in it held the biggest secret in the world. It arrived a week after she was killed—her ghost letter.

Before I read it, before I even opened it, I made myself say out loud that she was dead, she was still dead, that the letter did not change anything. Because it was so hard not to think that there had been some awful mistake that was about to be cleared up, finally. It was almost impossible not to hope, and so I made myself say it, again, that she was still dead, and then I opened the letter and read it, every word, devoured it like it was breath and I hadn't been breathing for a week. It was a regular letter, really, why wouldn't it be, she didn't know it would be her last, that someone would smash her head open later the same day.

Michael has moved our group along, moved us deeper into the prison building. I am still back at the bottom of the stairs, looking up to the most hated part of the prison, and thinking that what the guards did with the letters *was* torture.

We sit on benches in a big room inside the prison where the prisoners did their studying, had classes, where some of them learned to read. Some of the guards learned to read in this room, too—the prisoners taught them, and kept watch so the other guards wouldn't catch them getting taught by the prisoners. I think about telling Mom this story, how much she'll love it. And I swear I can feel it, that people have learned to read here—as if patience and trying can get soaked up into the walls of places. Mom should be here, I think. Laura *was* here. And here I am!

The best cells, Michael says, had a view of where the

boat came in and departed from the island. Children of the guards came out, sometimes, to visit their fathers, and the prisoners in those cells could see them: the children. He says that having your family taken away from you makes you hungry for so much, so that if you can see a child running out from a boat, playing, "then you feel like the luckiest somebody."

We have just come from seeing the cells, including #5, where Nelson Mandela lived for twenty-five years, with its bucket and folded blanket on the floor, his cage.

Michael tells us they fought for things that were worth fighting for: books, enough food so they didn't get sick, hot water. Not about every little injustice. They picked the battles that made a difference between living and dying.

I feel small and smaller, sitting here, listening to him. It's like big, important history drapes over everything here in South Africa—waiters and quarries and a president who had to live in a cage. Nothing I know comes close to being a matter of life and death, nothing I can think of. I remember how in third grade Mrs. Hogan had us make our own personal history books. We got to include all the stuff that marked what had happened in our lives so far. Almost everyone had learning to ride a bike, or moving, or a baby sister or brother being born. Grandparents dying, and dead animals, too—cats and dogs and gerbils. All the little stuff we thought was so important. But it *was* important to us! You can't help how and where you are born, what family you get, what country you live in!

When Michael invites us to ask questions, I want to, but I can't. Someone asks about the size of the prison population. Someone else wants to know how the prisoners got news of what was going on in the outside world. Finally the man next to me asks, "Aren't you bitter?" It is my father. "Why aren't you bitter?" A good, real question. I'm glad he asked it, proud.

Michael sighs deeply. Then he says, heavily, "No." It is a deep, final sound, his *no*. He says that being bitter will not help anything, will keep him from going forward. He says it is time to get on with other things, with reconciliation.

I believe him, but I don't get it. I look hard at him again, the way I did earlier, to see if spending half his life in prison shows on him, only this time I am looking for whatever it is that lets him not be bitter, and it does not show either; it must be on the inside. He tells us that he and some of the former prisoners still live on the island, together with some of their former jailers.

Michael stands at the door as we file out to board

the bus again and make our way back to the ferry. He shakes hands with each person in our group. I look him in the eye. I know this is stupid, but I try and put everything I think and feel into my handshake—my smallness, how I felt the reading in the walls of the classroom, how much I loved hearing him say "the luckiest somebody." It occurs to me that maybe his history gave him the chance to get bigger, and he took it.

On the ferry I get that wired feeling again—like I got in Soweto and after we talked to Phillip at dinner. Like things inside me are waking up, and grouchy. Like my toes feel when they start to thaw out after they've been all numb and cold, how much that hurts. I don't know what to do with everything. At least Dad doesn't ask me what I think or try to make me talk to him.

They show a National Geographic video about sharks for most of the ride back.

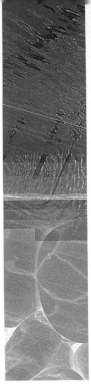

IN THE MORNING I LIE IN BED COUNT-
ing on my fingers how many days
we've been in South Africa—seven—
and how many days to go. Four. I feel
like we've been gone forever. It's definitely the longest Dad and I have
been together—just the two of us—
for probably our whole lives.

Today we're off to the wine country, to fill up the last
few days before the ceremony. I'm not up for it, making another switch, being in a whole new place with a
whole new load of things I'm supposed to be interested
in and appreciate.

Dad must think he's earned a little rest, though, at
whatever bed-and-breakfast he's booked us into for the
next two nights. Maybe the wine country is his payback
to himself for giving me the trip to Kruger; wine is his
part of the package. Fair enough, I guess, even though

Dad got to have the animals too and I won't exactly be sharing the wine.

He actually seems comfortable driving on the left side of the road, which is how they do it over here. I don't say so, but I'm impressed. I wouldn't want to try. I have my permit at home, but I'm in no hurry to get my license.

Last year, when Dad first moved back to Washington and heard that my midterm grades had all dropped, he suggested to Mom that they take away my permit. What a joke! I don't care one way or another when or whether I get my license. It's not like there's really any place I'm dying to go. I'm a hard girl to punish, I guess, along with being a hard girl to please.

It's a three-hour drive to where we're going. I could sleep, but I don't. I don't even doze. I sit and look and get out at all the designated scenic views that Dad stops at. I undo my seat belt and dutifully walk to the edge to see the trees or rolling land or whatever it is that makes something scenic.

It's getting hot. Of course we have air conditioning on the whole time, but each time we stop—for those views, or so I can pee—it's hotter than it was before, the sun is beating down more, we are farther from the ocean and any natural way of cooling things off.

It's not hot like Washington, D.C., though. Not yet. I hate the weather at home. How humid and horrible it gets. Heat weighs me down, makes everything inside me heavier. It's hard to get a light feeling about anything. Sometimes I feel like I can't breathe.

We reach the fancy little town we're going to with no problem, but Dad misses the turn for our bed-and-breakfast and we end up in the outskirts, driving by acre after acre of vineyard or open field. And then, suddenly, a squatter village—a country version of what we saw in Soweto, a whole little city of shacks. I think of Mary sitting on her cot. Dad says it must be where the vineyard workers live. He turns around and a few miles later we are back in town, on the street with all the cafés and restaurants and gift shops, and Dad finds the road he meant to take.

We sail through the stone pillars that mark the driveway of Rocky End Bed and Breakfast. A group of black men, workers, are gathered near one of the pillars. We kick up driveway dust in our rented car, and I feel embarrassed and white and rich.

As soon as we step out of the car and into the hot afternoon, a very blond, very tan woman dressed in tight white cotton pants and a shirt tied in a knot above her bellybutton comes out the door to greet us. I turn to Dad, and catch him pulling in his gut, straightening to his full height.

Blondie leads us into the main house and shows us around and gets us settled. It's like we've landed in some place out of a magazine, a million miles away from any place called Africa, all these chunky pine tables and cabinets and baskets and checkered napkins and pottery with tiny Dutch people in clogs painted all over them. It's Martha Stewart does Africa, only our Martha is named Suzanne and has a clipped little accent. I wonder if Martha has a Mr. Stewart somewhere, and where he is.

She makes sure that we have everything we could possibly need before she toodles back outside and across the driveway to the little cottage where she lives. But she's back again soon enough, to tell us what she forgot to mention: extra towels for the pool—"Oh, feel *free*, please *do* take a dip"—and sherry at five o'clock.

My room is perfect and seems kind of fake to me, like it isn't really meant to be *used*. I throw my stuff down on top of the bed and kick my shoes off. My country-curtained windows look out over the pool and gardens and a sloping, layered expanse of lawn. It really is beautiful, I don't know why I'm being such a bitch.

Probably because the heat has gone inside me. Even

the cool breeze in my room doesn't help. I have to go swim. The pool's not any bigger than the ones all over the hotel in Johannesburg, but I have got to get inside it, submerge. I put on my suit and walk down to the pool and straight into the water. I go under for a long time, not swimming forward, being under.

When I surface, I see a banged-up truck loaded with workers making its way down the winding driveway. I am a periscope, my head above the water, seeing them and not being seen. Their shirts, bright yellow and red and green, are fluttering like mad and I can see their teeth because they are laughing and smiling as they talk to each other, all jammed in the back of the truck together, looking awfully happy to be on their way out of here. I think of where they are going to, the place Dad and I saw getting here, and I want to believe they have someplace better to go to, but I know they don't. I watch them until they are out of my sight and the dust the truck whirled up has settled.

Then it's me and the water and it feels so good I can barely stand it. It makes me cry, almost. From missing it, I guess—from having been away from it and acting like I didn't care. I bob out to the deepest part and extend my arms and tread, lean back and cool off the crown of my head. Water is such a relief.

"How is it?" My father has appeared on the slate edging around the pool. I never even heard him or saw him coming.

"Oh," I say, jolting around to look at him. He is in his swimming trunks and that embarrasses me. I don't look at him for long, but I'm aware of his hairy chest, a bigger stomach than I remember him having, but when am I remembering from? When I was five, seven? When's the last time we were swimming together? I drop my arms in closer to my body. "It's good," I tell him. "Not too bathtubby."

"Well, it looked too inviting to pass up," he says. I hear him tossing his towel over to the lounge chair. "Suzanne says this is the first day it's really been warm enough."

I don't want him to join me. I don't want him to refer to Suzanne. I don't like that he is standing where he is, watching me in the water. "It's all yours," I tell him, making my way to the shallow end and the steps.

"Where you going?" he says. "You just got in."

This is true, Dad. "I already did my thousand laps," I say, and grab my towel and wrap it around my waist.

His shoulders slump. "What is it *now*, Berry?" he says.

I turn to him with such quickness, as if I am genuinely startled and confused by his question. "What?" I say, my word light as a breath, as if I can't possibly imagine what he's talking about. "Nothing," I say sincerely. "Really." It's shitty, what I'm doing, and I do it anyway. As I make my way back up to the house I hear him entering the water, pushing in, and then a little splash when he goes completely under.

Suzanne is out on the porch making a flower arrangement, choosing from cut flowers lying in a U-shaped basket. Now there's a job. She looks like a picture in a magazine. I think of my mother, sitting at the dining room table, paying bills, sipping cold coffee. I think of Mary, sitting on her cot in Soweto!

"Did that feel good?" Suzanne asks, holding a pink gladiola. She smiles at me as if I were my father. "Cool you off?"

"Yeah," I tell her, and I keep right on moving, straight through the double doors and into the tasteful tiled entryway, and then down the hallway to my little room, where I can close the door.

I flop across the bed and shut my eyes. I am missing something—or something is missing inside me— that's how it feels. What? Home? If I were there right now, I'd reach for my pile of stones.

• • •

Even without them I fall asleep, or come close enough to it that I feel little twitches running through my legs, and I startle awake at the sound of their voices—Dad's and Suzanne's. I can see them from my window. They are sitting on the lounge chairs by the pool under the white canvas umbrella. They each have a drink. She is pointing things out to him in the distance, gesturing with her arms. Probably explaining to him where everything is, where the best grapes grow. I swear I can hear her heavy gold bracelets jangling as she sweeps her arm back and forth along the horizon they're both pretending to be so interested in.

They don't have a clue how obvious they are.

I wonder if they'd sleep together tonight if I weren't here. If they will anyway.

When Laura died, a huge group of her Berkeley friends came to Washington for the funeral. Some of them stayed at the house with us, but everyone was there all the time anyway—the whole week was a mob scene.

One of her friends, Barb—someone we hadn't met before, but how could we have, Laura had a zillion friends—was this incredible person. She instantly fit right in and took over doing whatever needed to be done. She reminded me of Laura a little, how well she did everything. She picked people up at the airport, organized all the food neighbors brought over for meals. Whenever she was around me she touched me, and it was all right, I liked it. One night I saw her in the kitchen, scrubbing a pot and crying all by herself. Later that same night she actually got people singing. She was also beautiful.

Dad zeroed right in on Barb. I could see him kind of perk up whenever she came in the room. And at first I was glad for it because he was so crazed and manic the rest of the time I couldn't stand to look at him. But then it started to creep me out, how he would always go over and stand by her and get her to talk to him and offer her a drink. How, when she turned away to go do something, with so much sadness hanging over everything, he would still check out her ass.

I don't know if he creeped Barb out or not. She kept being who she was. But I hated it, how he was with her, so alert. On top of everything else that was going on, I worried that he wouldn't make it all the way through the funeral without actually hitting on her.

Dad and Suzanne have gone quiet. I look out the window and see they've left the pool. A minute later there's a knock on my door. It's Dad telling me that Suzanne has made reservations for us at a wonderful restaurant, highly recommended, for six o'clock. In his best imitation of offhand, he says, "I asked her to join us."

I bet you did.

"Hope that's all right with you," he says.

"Sure, why wouldn't it be?" I tell him, and he says a little before six, then, and closes my door.

Suzanne changes—but not enough!—for dinner. She is wearing a yellow dress with bold, well-placed designery flowers on it, and clip-clop white high-heel sandals.

I am wearing a dress, too—my one and only. I got it in Berkeley when I went out to visit Laura and Dad and Martina a few years ago. I found it in a consignment shop. It's two long, old-fashioned pillowcases that are stitched up the sides, with scoops for the neckline and arms. The lacy part hangs below my knees. I always like wearing this dress, how the soft white cotton feels. Like being between clean sheets, only standing up and walking. And there are slits so I don't have to take baby steps.

Dad is not pleased by my choice in clothing. Or shoes, my heavy boots. His face sets a little as soon as he sees me.

Suzanne says, "Oh, look at you! You beautiful young girls can wear anything." A compliment, I suppose.

"You could wear a paper bag and look great," she says.

"Don't give her ideas," my father says. *Her!*

Suzanne laughs.

My father turns to me. "Berry," he says. "Do you really think South Africa is ready for your haute couture?"

There is no way I am changing. None. "Oh, they can probably handle it, Dad," I tell him. "I mean, they handled *apartheid* for all those years ..."

Suzanne turns away and pretends not to have heard, and my father is pissed, but he instantly backs off about my dress. We look at each other, no blinking.

"Shall we?" he says and extends his arm toward the door. We file out, I am leading. No one can see my expression. At the car I pull open the back door. Suzanne says *Oh no no no, let me climb in back,* and I tell her it's fine, for her to get up front. This is all such bullshit.

Dad grips the headrest behind Suzanne's blond hair as he looks out the back window and steers the car out the driveway. Suzanne tells us that we are really taking our lives in our hands by going out on a Friday night. She sounds like she is confiding in us. "Payday," she says, nodding. "A little bit of money in hand, too much beer. They'll be falling down in the streets in a few hours," she says. "Really!" she adds, making her eyes big. "They *cannot* hold their liquor."

It takes me a second, an extra beat or two, to get what she is saying. Who *they* are. Her workers. Blacks. All blacks everywhere, every Friday night. Falling down in the street. Hundreds, thousands of them.

I am speechless—a funny feeling that's different from what usually keeps me quiet. No words come to me at all, even inside my head. Dad has turned the car around and is heading forward. I can't see his face. Suzanne is sitting sideways, looking at him, ready to chat about anything. Her lipstick is glossy. Dad is steering the car with all his might. I can feel him and me being embarrassed together, and *that's* weird, too.

At the restaurant—part of some local winery—Suzanne obviously knows all the people; everyone has little light kisses for each other, and they make a big deal about which table to give us. The glass-paneled dining room overlooks the wine cellar and we all go and stare at the barrels below, another scenic view.

Before we order, Suzanne starts in again: this time about the cheap wine *they* like to drink, and how absolutely undrinkable it is. She sounds so friendly, saying what she says, tossing it into the conversation like ground black pepper. This time I look at Dad and he is looking down, straightening his silverware and kind of nodding, like, yes, yes, let's go on, keep going.

• • •

And we do—or Suzanne and Dad do—go on, about all sorts of other things, but we keep coming back—who brings us, how does it happen?—to other awful things she has to say about *them*: how incapable they are of hard work, how unable they are to govern—*They don't even want to, really they don't!* After a while I stop holding my breath when she says something awful. *She's* certainly not embarrassed. She doesn't see how it changes things at the table, on our faces, how different the quiet is between words. How can she not feel *that?*

Dad keeps steering the conversation back toward wine. It's clearly a whole lot better for my father when he manages to keep her clear of politics. Poor Dad: an available hottie who turns out to be a racist. I could lean over and whisper to him that I know how he feels, kind of. *Every time Josh opens his mouth,* I could say, *something so stupid, so beside the point comes out of it.* But it's not the same, I know that. Not the same at all. How can Dad sit here and listen?

We haven't even had our salads. There's different wine for every bite. Suzanne makes sure to include me, to show Dad how good she is with children. She throws out questions and I answer. It is going to be a long night.

Her husband, it turns out, is in England, making the

bucks. "We can hardly afford to have all our eggs in one basket," she explains. "Given the economy here and where it's headed." It's clear she thinks it's going straight to hell. So her husband is off in London, and her two grown children are gone, too—one in the States, one in England. "There's nothing for them here," she informs us, sadly. "Absolutely nothing." And I think, Well, *you're* here, Suzanne. You must be a big part of the nothing.

They order a dessert wine and talk about what stupid grape it is. Since when did Dad become such a wine lover? Since he left, obviously, moved on. I remember Mom and him out on the deck, and they drank beer, or had soda along with Laura and me.

He and Suzanne have been swirling their glasses and sticking their noses in them all night. "Sure you don't want to try a sip?" Dad asks.

No thanks, I tell him. I'm sure.

Finally, finally, finally I am back in my room. Dad and Suzanne are out on the porch, keeping their voices low, but occasionally she laughs, full of all the wine she drank, and so I know they're there.

My bed is incredibly comfortable and there is a flower-scented breeze coming through the window and

if everything were completely different I would love it: the bed and the perfect weight of the silky sheet and the light blanket, how the air smells, the low murmur of their voices. I loved that, when I was little and Mom and Dad had friends over for dinner and I got to stay up late and then finally went off to sleep hearing them still talking and laughing. It gave me a good feeling I can still remember and that could even come over me now if I let it, but I tell myself not to, that this is completely different. That's the crummy work I'm doing—telling myself how different all this is—when I finally fall asleep, which is really the only place I've wanted to be all day.

By the time I come out of my room Dad is already up and at the table, reading a newspaper and eating fresh fruit. He looks showered and rosy and like all his clothes just got back from the dry cleaner's. I still have on my dress from last night, which I slept in. He says good morning and asks if I got a good night's sleep. Suzanne comes in with a basket of muffins and they start talking about our "options" for the day. Suzanne is a wealth of information.

I take my muffin and go out through the double doors, up into the orchard directly behind the house. Narrow paths run between the aisles of trees. The

ground feels good under my bare feet, and the sun feels good on my shoulders, not too much, not beating on me yet. I sit down underneath a tree and eat my breakfast here.

I can't stand to go back inside when I'm done, so I walk up farther into the orchard. I like the idea of walking away, for as long and far as I can go. I do two cartwheels in a row, straight down the path between the trees on my right and left. My dress accordions up toward my shoulders and then falls back into place when I stand up, and I can feel the blood pounding in my head. My dream from last night comes to me: I dreamed I had my long hair back. I had long hair the whole time I was growing up, before I started cutting it off, in stages, before I finally shaved my head. Now it's real, real short, growing in from bristly. I keep walking but finally turn back when the path seems to go on forever, this endless orchard.

As I approach the house I hear someone shouting. It's Suzanne, I realize, and she's mad. She sounds like she's lecturing a little kid, but I know it can't be hers—hers are grown and gone because there is nothing for them here, *nothing*. When I get beyond the orchard I see her, on the porch, lecturing a black woman with a gold and black scarf wrapped around her head. Suzanne is

pointing her finger at the woman as she speaks, as she *scolds* her. It's a horrible sight, and I freeze, embarrassed, but I am out in the open now, and it is only a second before Suzanne senses my presence and looks up to where I am. A bright smile breaks out across her tan face. "Welcome back!" she calls out, as if she's been waiting all morning to sing out to me, as if I've come upon her choosing cut flowers for an arrangement.

What do I do, wave? Smile? Spit? I jut my chin out to her in acknowledgment and start walking toward them. "Morning," I say, as I quickly step between them. Suzanne lightly touches my arm as I walk by. *"Plenty more food inside,"* she tells me. "Please help yourself."

"OK," I say. All I want to do is get by her.

"Did you have a nice walk?" she continues.

"Yeah," I say.

"It's a nice way to start off the day, isn't it? Your father tells me that you are quite a thinker." For a second I actually think she said "stinker." *Your father tells me you are quite a stinker.* But she said—he said—thinker.

"He wonders about what goes on in that mind of yours." She gives me this stupid conspiratorial smile like she's letting me in on a special secret we can share. *Just us girls.* I look at her, don't say a word. She keeps smiling her bright, toothy smile and gives me another pat on my arm. "Go eat," she says. "You're so thin and I'm so jealous!"

The regal woman in the gold and black headdress has been standing behind me, silent, the whole time. As I turn to go inside, I look at her and roll my eyes. I want her to know I hate Suzanne, too, that I'm not on Suzanne's side at all, that I'm sorry she has to stay and be yelled at like a bad kid, right out in the open. But the woman is not looking at me, or at Suzanne, or anything at all. She is staring slightly down, and far away, *gone*. She looks like I feel a lot of the time. And there isn't a chance she'll look at me and we'll connect. I am one of *them* to her, the same way she is one of *them* to Suzanne.

Dad is inside, making calls and doing business. When he gets off the phone he tells me the plan he and Suzanne cooked up—a tour of one of the wineries. "At two," he informs me.

"No thanks," I say. "I'll skip it."

He gets real quiet, and when Suzanne comes in, offering coffee, he says the plan may not work out after all. "Problem?" she says, neatly, as she pours.

Dad tells her that I'm not sure I want to go wine tasting.

I'm sure. Didn't I sound sure? Isn't *no* a sure word?

Dad and Suzanne take the conversation and run with it. Perhaps there's something else I'd enjoy more, perhaps later in the afternoon, Suzanne has a friend with a daughter about my age ... They talk to each other, *about* me. I watch them. It comes around to me maybe staying here while they go out. Suzanne is visiting the winery too, apparently. Did Dad say that?

Every part of their conversation infuriates me: that they're even having this discussion—what am I, some baby who can't be left alone for one second?—and that *they're* having this discussion. It's the kind of conversation parents have, a mother and father. Not father and wanna-be lover, or father and racist, or father and some woman who means nothing, less than nothing, to me.

Maybe Dad will pick this moment to tell her about Laura, about what happened to her, how she died, the rock that hit her head and broke it apart, so that she'll understand his concern about leaving me alone, so that she'll sympathize. Oh God, I can see her—reaching out her jangly arm to touch him. "Oh, Myles," she'll say. "How horrid. Horrid!" How it will make them feel so together, so connected: to share this moment, this memory of such inconceivable loss (that's what the minister said at the service, I remember that now: *inconceivable loss*). Suzanne may cry. At least her eyes will fill up, they'll make her blue eyes—are they blue? or green?—bluer, or greener, whatever they are. It'll be pretty, this almost crying. And Dad will be strong, silent. They'll take a moment before they tiptoe back to what's really up for them: wine tasting, what to do with me, how they can arrange this. They'll work their way around to exactly what they want, but carefully.

And when they do decide to go, I tell them of course it's fine, no problem. They leave the phone number of the vineyard they'll be visiting and tell me what time they will be back, like I'm the babysitter *and* the baby. "We won't be gone long," my father emphasizes. Liar. They both want to be out of here, on their way: it's so obvious.

When I went out to visit Laura at Berkeley—Dad had moved to California to live with Martina by then—Dad and Martina and Laura and I all had dinner together at a restaurant in San Francisco. It was the first place I'd been to where they had olive oil for the bread instead of butter. Martina brought me a present—just for meeting me, like my existence was some sort of happy occasion. It was one of those hand-painted silk scarves, clearly not cheap, something I would never, under any circumstances, ever wear. I actually have a box at home, a collection of things Dad's girlfriends have given me. I have this idea to do an art project out of it, some kind of still life, if I ever get around to it.

After dinner, lying around back in Laura's dorm, we laughed about how completely wrong Martina was for him and mocked her dopey glasses and the way she kind of folded her body in against Dad's. I said Martina was a front anyway, that Dad had really moved out to California to be near Laura.

Laura's smile erased. She sat up and shook her head. "No," she said. "No, he didn't. He moved here to be with his girlfriend."

It was one of those completely crummy moments, because we both knew that what she said was true. Laura was his favorite—there was no doubt about that, and Laura never tried to pretend like she wasn't—but even being his favorite didn't count for all that much. Dad didn't move to California to be near Laura, like he didn't stick around Washington to be with me. It was so obvious he and Martina were never going to last—he was done with her in less than a year—but she was what he wanted right then, and that's why he was where he was.

Fine, then, go! *Go!* I want to be alone and away from you, too.

When they leave I stand on the porch and wave good-bye to them, *good riddance to bad rubbish*—that pops into my head from a million years ago, saying it to Laura when she wouldn't take me somewhere with her and I was mad. But their being gone actually makes an instant, awful difference. The place feels empty and creepy and I feel alone, except for whoever is in the kitchen chopping things, and whoever is pruning in the orchard, snip snip, and whoever is mowing the lawn down to its nub. Such a heaviness comes over me—as if all the stones I've collected over the months have gone inside me, slid through some trapdoor in my flesh and bones—stones in my heart, my heart a stone. And inside me, it all weighs too much.

I walk down to the pool and stand outside it and look at the water. If I go in I will not be able to float. I will sink. I go back up to the house. Inside, the cart of liquor in the corner of the dining room catches my eye, a little altar, kind of, with its pretty arrangement of bottles. It's loaded: gin, bourbon, vodka, dark liqueur bottles with fake gold screw-tops, and a silver ice bucket with tongs beside it. As I walk by I step in a little closer and grab one of the bottles, I don't bother to see which one, I just wrap my hand around its tall neck and take it with me into the bedroom. I got gin. It's a frosty bottle, about three-quarters full, and I unscrew the top and take a sip. Not a glug, because I know that whatever it tastes like is going to be a surprise, and I may not like it, I may cough it right back up. So it's a sip and it doesn't taste good at all, but it doesn't make me sick, either. I take another one, and then screw the top on and return it to its spot on the cart, right where it belongs. I don't know what to do next. I can't swim, I don't want to be inside. I walk back out.

I go down by the pool and lie in the sun. I don't feel much of anything. When it gets too hot, I move under the umbrella. But moving takes so much energy. The sun gives me a headache and all I want to do is sleep.

But I can't. Thoughts keep coming, making their way in. And everything I think about is stuff that has already happened, that I can't do anything about. There is all this garbage stuck in my mind, and it keeps me from going to sleep, and besides, I keep hearing noises.

Not the mowing or the snipping. These are different noises, and I don't know what they are or where they are coming from, and they scare me, all the cracks and rustles. Every once in a while one is louder than another and I jolt forward and sit up and look around. But there is nothing, no one. I am alone.

I lie back down and close my eyes, but it happens again, whenever I start to drift off: another little sound or rustle, and I shoot up, alert. To what? Who's there? What am I afraid of?

Men. That's who I'm afraid of. Black men, the ones I think are hiding behind the bushes, beyond the garden, on the slope of the land, or up in the orchard, behind every tree. With tools: rakes, clippers, scythes, submachine guns. Smiling, white teeth, bouncy. Mad. Filled up with hate and waiting to come and kill me.

I am sitting up, frozen and listening. I hear a bird. I hear the filter in the pool click on, the churning of it. I am so scared I can hardly make my body move, but I have to. I have to go inside, away from everything, and close the door, but I stumble as I climb off the canvas-covered recliner.

Now I am walking fast and holding myself back from running at the same time. When I reach the house I pull the door closed behind me and it slams and it's all I can do not to cry.

I go over to the liquor cart and take another sip—of something else, from a different bottle. This one tastes like nothing, flavored nothing—and as I'm putting the bottle back in place, I have an urge to set it down way too heavily, to really smack it hard so that it cracks and so that the bottles next to it shatter and the ones around them fall over like slow bowling pins.

I don't, though. I put it back down carefully, where it belongs, and then I go into my bedroom, my little home-away-from-home, and pull on my black rayon drawstring pants. Then I hit the mattress with my fist and it gives beneath my punch, of course, and so I turn and hit the pine nightstand, hard, and it, being wood, *doesn't* give, and a jolt of pain shoots through my hand and up my arm. It comes out my mouth. I yell, hard, loud, pounding the nightstand again, then the windowsill. I pound everything around me that I can, and I keep hollering, all the time I'm pounding, for a long time before I finally get quiet.

I haven't been quiet for very long when I hear them—my father and Suzanne, home already, back so soon.

I step out of my room as Dad walks into the house. The first thing he says when he sees me is, "What happened?"

"*Nothing* happened," I hiss at him, stopping him in his tracks. "*Nothing!*" I want that expression wiped off his face right now, this instant—that terror that I've been hurt or scared, that something horrible happened while he was gone.

My hissing stops him and changes the look on his face—he is evaluating now, gauging where I am and how he must proceed.

I might explode. I might.

"Do you want to talk about it?" he asks, carefully.

"Talk about what, Dad? *What?*" I am yelling at him.

Suzanne chooses this moment to make her entrance and in a second is stopped cold by what she has walked in on. "Oh," she says, "excuse me, terribly sorry," and she turns, and pulls the door closed behind her as she steps outside, leaving Dad and me alone again.

"Terribly sorry," I say—a perfect imitation of her accent. I say it again, only this time I'm even chirpier: "*Ter*ribly sorry!" I realize I could say this over and over and over.

Dad is watching me like I am dangerous. His jaw muscle quivers, then sets. He waits.

I raise my eyebrows at him, give a little smile. I walk around to one of the beautifully upholstered chairs in front of the fireplace and plop down. As I drop into the seat cushion, it exhales a little whoosh and I lose my stomach for a second and all of a sudden it hits me: the alcohol—I'm drunk. Then I get scared, because I know if Dad finds out he will think *this* is what happened, this explains everything, why I am acting this way, saying these things that I am going to say. And that isn't so, it isn't true. I straighten myself up in the chair, plant my feet on the tiles, get control of all my face muscles.

"Are you all right, Berry?" he asks.

"Yes," I tell him. Straight and clear.

"What is it, then?" he asks.

I look at my father. He is nicely dressed. All the materials on him, his shirt and his pants, hang nicely on him, no wrinkles.

"What is it?" I repeat his question. It's a good question, after all. Well, I think, whatever it is is very painful. And it's not Laura. "It's not Laura," I say.

"OK," he answers evenly, coming around to sit on the ottoman in front of me. He is being careful not to say too much. I can tell that he wants me to keep going.

"I hate ..." I start, and then I stop, because I don't know what to say first—this trip, you and Suzanne, you, my life.

He is nodding now. He means *Go on.*

I start again. "What are we doing?" I say. I think, this is all bullshit. "Why are we doing this?"

Now that there is a question he has to answer he stiffens up more. "Why are we on this trip?" he asks. "Why did we come to South Africa?"

All right, that'll do. I nod.

He considers. "Well, I was under the impression that we came for the memorial ceremony—a chance for you and me to be together—in honor of Laura." He pauses, then starts again, a full confession: "My business, I had business, but that was secondary." He stops. "Is that what you meant, what you're asking me?"

"And what are *you and me* supposed to do?" I ask him. "What's *that* about?"

He doesn't get it. Neither do I. But he hates not getting it. "Berry," he says, "maybe it would be better if you said what you have to say, what's on your mind. I'm not quite sure what you want from me."

I go back to how I started all this: *I hate* ... and it is still hanging in the air where I left it, and it comes back to me, fills me. "This is all wrong," I say. "What we're doing, and why we're here, and how we're pretending everything's all right." He watches me. I am not getting through, saying what it is. "I," I start. "I don't ... I can't stand..." Nothing I try to say gets finished. "I hate *words*," I say finally. "For starters," I add. I hate them for not helping me enough, not saying anything that is the same as how I feel inside.

My father nods, as if he is a little relieved, or agrees with me some, and then he says, "They're all we have sometimes, and often insufficient."

I am shaking, trembling, my insides getting to my outside.

"Berry," my father says, and he leans over and puts his big hand on my knee, and it jolts me, his heavy hand.

I start to cry again. Boo hoo hoo.

This is it: the flood, the big meltdown. I kind of can't believe I have it in me—didn't I just *do* this? But this is another wave altogether, gathering inside and pouring out of me, spilling out my eyes, slithering down my nose, catching in my throat on its way out my mouth. Not pretty. And no stopping. I cry and cry and cry, and somewhere inside it all, my father kneels down in front of me and wraps his arms around me.

He rocks me—has been rocking me—because when I finally come out of it, the tidal wave, I am moving back and forth and realize that I *have* been for a long time. I finally stop but then I shudder and let out a cluster of hiccups.

God, what a mess.

I pull back from my father's chest. That's when I see the number I've done on his shirt, the tears and snot all over the silky folds of his shirt. And then I look at his face, and his shirt is nothing. God, does he look sad. As sad as the day he told me about Laura and his pants were shaking and he was so crumpled. And I know that he's looking that way now because of *me*, and that *I* look that way, too. We're mirrors of each other, and I can't not see myself in his face. But I don't want to! I do not want this connection, to see how related we are.

I take a deep breath in and out. Again and again. My father eases himself back onto the ottoman in front of me. I don't have a clue where to go from here. Now my head really hurts. "Suzanne is such a racist," I say.

He looks surprised at what I've said, but he adjusts pretty quickly. "Yes," he says, "she is."

"And you let her say all that stuff. It's disgusting."

I can tell he is one beat away from asking me if this is really what I want to be talking about—Suzanne's racism—but I have to hand it to him: he knows to follow my lead.

"It's the way she sees the world," he says. "Her world. It's not my place to come in and tell her she's got it all wrong."

"Why not?" I say. "You do with me."

He kind of smiles, because I kind of smiled when I said what I said. "I'm your *father*," he says.

"No kidding."

"I'm *supposed* to watch out for you and try and help you."

"Keep me on track," I say.

"That, too. If I can."

"At your convenience," I say.

"Pardon?"

"You watch out for me and keep me on track at your convenience," I say. "When it fits into your schedule. When you don't have something better to do."

He tightens away from me, but not totally. He is trying to stay where he is, sitting on the ottoman, close to me. "What can I say, Berry? I don't know what to say. You are so angry about so many things. I don't know where to begin."

I don't say anything more. I am trying to stay where I am, too, next to him.

"I'm not unaware of the ways I have failed you," he says. "Or most of the people I have tried to love, for that matter," he adds. "My leaving ..." he starts, but cannot finish. He brings his hands together and raises them up to his chin, which is quivering. "I do the best I can," he says, "and clearly, often, it is not enough."

I have stopped breathing. I cannot believe what I am hearing, his words that are coming to me. They are so shocking that they freeze me, kind of. And the first thing I know, when I can know anything, is that I want him to stop. "OK," I say, quickly. So he won't go on. I do not want, or need—I cannot stand—to hear more. "OK," I say again. *This* is enough, for right here and now, what he is saying, has said.

"OK?" he says. I see how much he wants to be off the hook, for this to be over, but he wants for me to really mean it, too.

"Yes," I tell him. I even put my hands on his knees. Then I use them to push myself up to standing. "I think we've had enough for one night," I tell him, and it's a relief for both of us to laugh. "Sorry about your shirt," I say, and he looks down and then up and tells me it's not a problem.

I more or less pass out on my bed, but I don't sleep through the night. I wake up into a dark, late, quiet part of the night. I don't know what wakes me up. There aren't noises and I'm not scared. I'm not even angry. I actually feel pretty empty, close to hungry. Finally it dawns on me, like a leaf landing on my arm, that I'm sad. That's it, that's all: I am sad, and it's a relief—to be sad, with nothing else besides that, no bomb underneath it, nothing covering it over. At least it doesn't weigh a ton.

And I'm awake, so I lie here with it. After a while I sit up in bed and look outside my window to the pool, which casts an eerie, beautiful glow into the night. I get out of bed and tiptoe my way down to the water. There are little guiding lights built into the sides of the slate pathway; I feel like I'm following a miniature landing strip. I stand outside the pool for a few seconds, looking in, before I pull off the T-shirt I was sleeping in and quietly step into the water. It's cold, but I don't let that stop me. I go all the way under, let my hands rise up over my head. Then I rise up to the surface, roll over, float.

Not for long. But long enough to get the floating feeling, the lightness. Then I walk out of the pool, dry myself a little with my shirt, and put it over me. I go back into my room and hop in between the sheets and curl up, warm my hands between my legs. I sleep for a few hours and when I wake up I feel clean.

I can hear my father and Suzanne in the dining room, talking. By the time I come out of my room for breakfast Dad has already loaded up the car. He's tapping: his fingers, his foot when he sits down. We're shy and quick saying good morning to each other. He is clearly ready and eager to be on our way, and he's being kind of formal with Suzanne, as if they haven't been hitting on each other for the last couple of days. I spoon marmalade onto my toast.

Suzanne is wearing a matching shorts-and-shirt set, with the collar of her shirt turned up and perky. She asks what kind of juice I'd like—orange, grapefruit, cranberry. I tell her no thanks, nothing, the toast is fine. "Pineapple?" she says. "Apple?" Finally, "Prune."

"Really," I say, "nothing," and retreat to my room to pack up my stuff. When I come back, my father is writing a check for what we owe her. I carry my backpack out to the car and Suzanne joins me. As soon as we are alone together, she says she certainly hopes I'll be able to enjoy the rest of our holiday.

I snort. Our holiday.

"Oh, did I say something funny?" she asks, stopping abruptly and fixing her big eyes on me. "*Do* let me in on the joke."

I blush, despite myself, and almost apologize. But why should I, to her? "We're not on vacation," I say, and look at her, clear and steady, for the second it takes to get it straight that we do not like each other, and then my father comes walking out of the house, pulling the sliding door closed behind him, putting on his sunglasses.

He walks over to where Suzanne and I are standing by the car. He reaches out his hand as if for a handshake but she steps in a little closer and he wraps his arm around her shoulder, squinches up her tan skin into a tight little wrinkled wad. "Thanks for everything," he says. They are both smiling, and Dad has made this little gesture, is saying thanks again, but I can see that he's only going through the motions. He is already gone, he's out of here, and Suzanne is still smiling up into his face and she thinks they're together. What a dope.

It makes me a little sick to see, though. It makes me jumpy inside, panicky almost. I want to warn her, or call out to Dad to stop it, but of course I don't. We climb into our rental car, and we go.

We pull out of the driveway and Suzanne stands waving in the dust the car kicks up around her. I turn back and look at her and all of a sudden I feel sorry—*terribly* sorry—for her, standing there, in the cloud we have stirred up. Sympathy for Suzanne, Miss Racist, Martha Stewart, for this woman we are leaving behind forever and who means nothing at all to my father, nothing.

I turn around in my seat and yank the seat belt across me and fasten myself in. I can't believe all the junk there is, in every single day, even the ones that start out like they might be OK. I don't want to feel sorry for Suzanne, I don't want to feel anything at all for her. It's not like she *loved* my father or Dad loved *her*, so even if he fails the people he loves, she isn't one of them. I am. I *am*!

Still, I look back one more time, to make sure that she has finally given up and gone inside. She has. Then I look at my father. Man-on-a-mission is staring straight ahead. He does not even check the rear-view mirror. He doesn't have a clue about anything that has gone on: Suzanne biting me, me biting her back, his leaving people in the dust. It's almost impressive, how out of it he can be.

I shake my head, and a little snort—part of it a laugh—escapes me.

My father looks over. "What?" he says.

I shake my head again. I'm about to say *Nothing*, but I stop myself. "Remember Sammy?" I say.

"Sure," he says. "Of course I remember Sammy."

Sammy was our dog. He used to chase our car whenever we drove off. It killed me, how far he would follow us, how hard he would run, until his tongue flapped sideways out his mouth. Even when he was old and filled with arthritis, he still chased our car, like he just couldn't get over that he didn't get to go along. I was always so relieved when I looked back and he had finally given up.

My father glances over at me. "What about him?"

"What a great dog he was," I say.

My father smiles. "Not a blistering genius," he says, "but a great dog."

 WE GET BACK TO CAPE TOWN and check into our hotel and we're tired. But it finally seems OK to do nothing, to watch a video and order hamburgers from room service. The ceremony is tomorrow, and we're not acting like it isn't.

I ask Dad if I can make a call.

He tells me sure, to go ahead.

I catch Mom as she's on her way out to some school event. "Berry!" she says to me. "Thank God!"

There is nothing wrong, she is just so glad I called. She doesn't say anything about feeling alone, even when I tell her that it feels like we've been gone forever but it's almost over. My voice sounds real to me, not chipper and not dead, somewhere in between. I tell her that we went to the wine country and had dinner with a real live racist, that Dad and I are doing OK.

We don't talk for long, but it is enough. I'm ready to sleep.

Dad pops in to see if I am still on the phone. "How's everyone?" he asks.

"Fine," I tell him. "Mom's fine."

"Josh?" he asks.

No Josh.

Dad and I both get up early but we stay in our rooms.

I put on and take off all the clothes I brought with me, every T-shirt and pair of pants, my pillowcase dress, every piece of jewelry. The whole heap of them is next to me, on the floor, and I am naked, and now it is really hitting me, this thing we are about to go do, and how much I don't want to do it. I'm sure all the stones are back in my heart, but I can't feel them. I can't feel anything.

Dad knocks on my door and tells me the time. I tell him I'm getting ready. How do you get ready? It's not about getting dressed.

On the drive to the school we are both quiet. Mostly I feel how dressed-up Dad is, how clean and crisp. I feel a little sick to my stomach, I can't remember why we are doing this. Didn't we already have a funeral and a service and a reception? Didn't it go on forever? And here we are again, like once was not enough! We don't even hit red lights on the way to the school.

We go directly into the church for the prayer service before the unveiling ceremony in the courtyard. Dad and I walk up the aisle and sit in the front pew, and a few minutes later the kids start to file in. I can hear them all, rustling around and getting settled. I don't want to turn and look at them, these kids who knew Laura, so I stare straight ahead, at the altar. I could pretend I'm praying and close my eyes, but I don't.

Father Alan prays, and a few of the kids get up and read from the Bible, and I stand and sit and kneel when everyone else does. Did Laura do all this church stuff when she was over here, did she start to believe in *this*, too? She never wrote about God stuff, I don't think, or if she did I'm pretty sure she didn't call it God. I am still trying to remember what she said, when the prayers come to an end and it is time to go. We file outside and the brightness is painful.

My father and I and Father Alan and Mr. Watanya, who is a teacher at the school and the artist who made the memorial to Laura, walk to the parched square of cement and dirt between the school and the church. All the kids are filing out behind us, making a semicircle around the memorial stone, which is covered by a canvas tarp in the center of the yard. More and more kids keep coming, and I can feel myself wanting them to stop, all these people who knew Laura, who *had* her, like there isn't enough room or air for all of us. Now I can't help but look at them—the kids—all these wiry, big-eyed kids looking right back at me. There is not a cloud in the perfectly blue sky.

As soon as everyone is there, a song erupts out of nowhere. There doesn't seem to be anybody leading it. Mr. Watanya walks over to the memorial and lifts a corner of the tarp, holding it in his fist until the song comes to an end. He is wearing a shirt full of flowers, and flashes a bright smile, eager to show what he has made.

Once there is silence, he pulls back the tarp and reveals a huge bowl—or dish, or vase—poured out of cement, maybe, but with so many stones and pieces of mirror stuck into the cement that it looks like they *are* the bowl. Some of the stones have swashes of blue paint across them, a beautiful sky blue. You can tell that someone, some real person with *hands*, made it—this bowl or dish or whatever is before us. This art. The whole piece is thick and kind of rough, and it's big—big enough that I could climb inside it along with a couple of the kids who are standing next to it. But it's not huge or shiny like the gross monuments all over Washington. What I'm seeing feels just right for what and where it is. Slivers and specks of mirror chips catch the sun and shoot out streaks of light. There is *nothing* dead about it, nothing. And I love it.

I *love* it.

Another song starts up. No one I can see is leading it, and this time there's clapping.

All of a sudden I feel Laura herself so strongly that it actually jolts my body. It's incredible how complete a wave of her—herself, who she was—comes over me, passes through me, and then I miss her, I miss her so much I don't know if I can keep standing up. Maybe I sway or teeter or something, because the next thing I know Father Alan has his arm around my shoulder and is pulling my body in against his, which is moving along with the music. And so I do that, too—move to the music—instead of falling down. I look at Dad and tears are *streaming* down his face, he is crying away and not even brushing them off.

Everyone is singing and clapping and Dad is crying and I am moving to the music instead of falling down, and it is only a moment, but I *know* that it is big.

. . .

I don't want it to, but the song ends. Now Mr. Watanya is reading the plaque that is set into the ground next to the memorial. He reads words, and dates—the dates of Laura's life—and he reads that she was a friend to this school and to South Africa. We clap and then he is done, and it is quiet. All that matters to me is that what they made out of stones and mirrors is beautiful. But then I realize that Dad and Father Alan are looking at me, everyone is looking at me, as if it is my turn to do something.

The check! I have the check in my hand, I have scrunched up my fist around it and it is my turn to do my part. I hold it up, and then extend my arm toward Father Alan, who is to my right. It is so clumsy a gesture, so abrupt, that even *I* can't stand it, and I draw my arm down and back. I can't say, "Here. Here's the money."

I look at Father Alan. Everyone is waiting. My father takes a small step forward. He is going to speak if I don't.

"Laura was my sister," I blurt out, suddenly. I barely recognize my own voice and I don't know where the words are coming from, or what I am going to say.

"And I loved her." I hear those words come out of me. So I've started. Now what? What else is there, besides whatever connection there is? All the kids are looking at me.

"When she died," I say, "I couldn't believe it! Because the thing Laura was always the most was *alive!*" But I believe now, I do. Death made me a believer.

"Laura was a big believer. She believed in how you all are changing your country. She loved South Africa," I say. "Where people were willing to die for what they believe in."

I really don't have a clue what comes next, after being a believer. But everyone is still looking at me, listening, as if I have something to say.

"Why am I telling *you?*" I ask. "This is *your* country, where *you* live, where *you've* lost people you love." I think of Phillip, his brothers. A few of the kids are nodding, and now a few more. Father Alan, too, nodding naturally, like I have said a simple, true thing. Like I have said the sun is shining and it *is* shining. "So it's not like we're alone in this," I say, and a pebble falls to where it wants to be, inside me.

"And it must have seemed unbelievable to you, too, to lose someone you loved who was good and only wanted what was right. Who maybe you didn't get to say good-bye to, or thank you, or I'm sorry." Oh, God. What am I *doing?* Where am I *going* with this?

"I have a check here," I say, starting over. I raise my hand. "It's only money. We collected it at home—*my* home, where I live. By swimming! We raised it by swimming laps in a pool that we have at our school." All of a sudden this seems like an important thing to say, to make clear. Like: *This is the toilet the squatters use. This is how they tightened the bag. I have failed those I've tried to love.* To simply say what is. *My name means the king.*

"We had a swimathon, where people—students—swam a long time and other people donated money." It sounds so ridiculous! "We didn't know what else to do."

And that's really the truth, isn't it? So much of the time we don't know what to do.

"But we wanted to do something—to keep the connection that Laura made with all of you and with this place. That she loved."

Oh, can I be done? Is this enough? Maybe it is: I'm back to love. *Love, Laura*—the way she wrote it, in all her letters home, in her last letter home, sitting in the table next to my bed, underneath my pile of stones.

"So thank you," I say. "For being here, and part of everything, thank you very much—for letting us be part of everything with you." I turn and give the check to Father Alan and he wraps me in an enormous hug.

I'm finally done—or begun. I hope!